Love and Loyalty

*A Felicity Classic
Volume 1*

by Valerie Tripp

★ AmericanGirl®

Printed in China
17 18 19 20 21 22 23 LEO 9 8 7 6 5 4 3 2 1

Cover image by David Roth and Juliana Kolesova;
© iStock.com/flownaksala (background); © iStock.com/Zuzule (horse)

Cataloging-in-Publication Data available from the Library of Congress

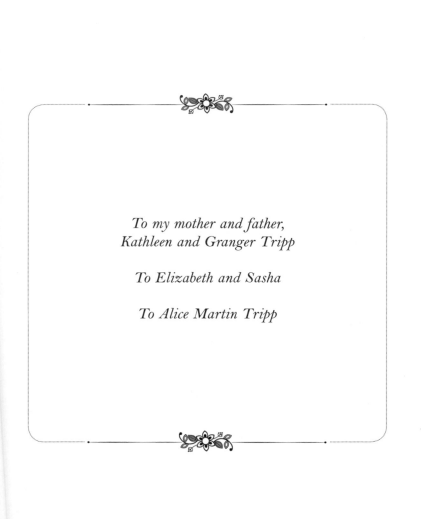

To my mother and father,
Kathleen and Granger Tripp

To Elizabeth and Sasha

To Alice Martin Tripp

Beforever™

The adventurous characters you'll meet in
the BeForever books will spark your curiosity
about the past, inspire you to find your voice
in the present, and excite you about your future.
You'll make friends with these girls as you share
their fun and their challenges. Like you, they are
bright and brave, imaginative and energetic,
creative and kind. Just as you are, they are
discovering what really matters: Helping others.
Being a true friend. Protecting the earth.
Standing up for what's right. Read their stories,
explore their worlds, join their adventures.
Your friendship with them will BeForever.

TABLE *of* CONTENTS

Merriman's Store

Felicity Merriman pushed open the door to her father's store and took a deep breath. She loved the smell of coffee beans and chocolate, of pine soap, spice tea, and apples. No other place in the world smelled as good as her father's store.

"Good day, Mistress Merriman!" said her father. He smiled and bowed.

Felicity grinned. Her father always pretended she was a fine lady customer when she came to his store. "Good day, Mr. Merriman," she answered. She liked to pretend, too.

"That's a lovely hat you are wearing, young miss. Have you come to buy a new feather for it?" said Mr. Merriman. "Or perhaps you'd like some new ribbon or straw flowers?"

"Oh, Father! You know I don't fancy this old hat at

all," giggled Felicity. "I wear it only because Mother insists." She pushed the straw hat off her head so that it hung down her back.

"Aye," agreed her father. "It's supposed to shade your face, so that the sun does not make your nose red."

Felicity rubbed her nose. It *was* rather pink. "I do forget to wear my hat sometimes," she said.

Mr. Merriman smiled. "Sometimes you forget and sometimes you are in too much of a hurry. I know my impatient girl. But don't fret. I think your nose is very pretty indeed." He tapped Felicity's nose with the tip of his finger. "And now, tell me. What did your mother send you to fetch today?"

Felicity stood very tall and pretended to be a fine lady again. "A penny's worth of ginger root, if you please, sir."

Her father bowed. "Yes, madam. Ginger it is," he said. "And here's a bit of rock candy for your trouble."

"Thank you, Father," said Felicity. She popped the candy in her mouth and tasted its sharp sweetness. While her father weighed the ginger root and wrapped it in newspaper, Felicity looked around the store. The shelves were crowded with bolts of cloth, bowls, bottles, kettles, and coffee pots. Fat-bellied sacks of rice, flour, and salt leaned against barrels of nails.

Everywhere Felicity looked, she saw something useful or pleasing. There were aprons, night-caps, combs, spices, sponges, rakes, fishing hooks, tin whistles, and books. Felicity loved to daydream about the faraway places everything came from. The tulip bulbs came from Holland, the tea from China, and the cotton from India. Felicity believed her father's store was the finest store in Williamsburg and probably the finest store in all the thirteen colonies. The King of England himself didn't go to a better shop in London, Felicity was sure.

Mr. Merriman handed Felicity a neatly wrapped packet. "Here is your ginger, Lissie," he said. "Put it safe in your pocket so you won't lose it the way you lost the sugar last week."

Felicity put the ginger deep in her pocket. "I didn't quite *lose* the sugar, Father," she said. "I gave it away."

"To a horse!" laughed Mr. Merriman. "Ah yes, now I remember." He winked at his daughter. "I believe you'd give a horse anything. You do love horses, don't you, Lissie?"

"Aye!" said Felicity, nodding happily.

Mr. Merriman patted Felicity's pocket. "Mind you, don't give this ginger to any horse, or I'll be very disappointed. I'm hoping it's meant for a cake to go with my supper this evening. Hurry along home now, so you can help bake my ginger cake."

"Oh, must I go home, Father?" asked Felicity. Baking a ginger cake at home was not as interesting as helping in the store. Felicity loved to greet customers. Sometimes Father let her help them choose buttons and ribbons to buy. Sometimes she helped Marcus count the boxes and barrels of goods that had come in on ships from England. "May I stay here for a while?" Felicity asked. "May I help Marcus in the storeroom?"

"No, Lissie, you needn't stay," said Mr. Merriman. "Have you forgotten? Ben helps Marcus in the storeroom now."

Hmph! thought Felicity. *Ben is so quiet and shy, 'tis easy to forget him.* Ben was the new apprentice. Father was teaching him how to run a store. Ben had come to live with the Merrimans one month ago. He slept in the loft above the stable and mostly kept to himself. Ever since Ben had come, Mr. Merriman did not need help in the store at all.

Felicity sighed. She knew where she *should* be helping—at home. A pile of mending was waiting for her
there. Felicity hated the idea of sitting straight and still,
stitching tiny stitches, when all the while she was stiff
with boredom. She would much rather stay at the store.
But her father had already turned back to his work.
There was nothing to do but go home.

Felicity was in luck. Just as she opened the door to
go out, a stout, well-dressed lady sailed in. The lady's
hat was decorated with ribbons and feathers that fluttered like leaves in a breeze. Felicity stepped back and
held the door open wide.

"Mrs. Fitchett!" said Mr. Merriman happily. "What
a pleasure! I haven't seen you since summer began. You
look well!"

"Thank you, thank you, sir," said the lady cheerily.
"You are looking well yourself." She nodded toward
Felicity. "And who is this pretty maid?" she asked. "It's
not your little Lissie, is it?"

Felicity smiled as her father answered, "Indeed, it is
Felicity."

"Well, well!" Mrs. Fitchett gasped as if she were
surprised. "The dear girl! Grown so tall and pretty! Hair

as bright as a marigold! I am sure *she'll* have the lads flocking about, Mr. Merriman." Mrs. Fitchett turned to Felicity. "Are you ready for the lads to come a-courting, Miss Felicity? Are you working on your sampler of stitches to show them how well you sew?"

"No, ma'am," said Felicity. "I've not begun a sampler as yet."

"Not yet?" Mrs. Fitchett asked. "Why my two girls had finished their samplers when they were your age!"

"My Lissie's not much of a one for stitching," said Mr. Merriman. "She hasn't the patience."

"High-spirited, is she?" said Mrs. Fitchett. "Well, well, Mr. Merriman. Your girl will find her patience when she goes looking for it, I'm sure. Wait till she meets a fellow she fancies. She'll settle down fast enough."

"Lissie is far more interested in horses than fellows," smiled Mr. Merriman. "She'd rather go for a horseback ride than go to a fancy-dress ball." He looked at Felicity. "Isn't that true, Lissie, my girl?"

"Of course, Father!" said Felicity. She did not believe anyone could prefer dancing to riding horses.

"Horses!" exclaimed Mrs. Fitchett. "That reminds

me why I came to your store today. I want to order oats
for our horses to eat. Will you have your man bring a
sack of oats 'round to my house, Mr. Merriman?"

"I'll have my new apprentice do it," said Mr. Merriman. "Ben is going to deliver a new bit and bridle to
Jiggy Nye at the tannery this afternoon. He will bring
the oats to your house on his way."

"Very well," said Mrs. Fitchett. She lowered her
voice to a gossipy tone. "I know why that good-for-
nothing Jiggy Nye wants a new bridle and bit. I hear
he's got himself a new work horse. He won it gambling
or some such thing. In any case, he didn't pay for it,
mind you."

Felicity listened closely. She wanted to hear more
about Mr. Nye's new horse. But Mrs. Fitchett frowned
and said, "I believe he worked his old horse to death.
That man is a cold-hearted scoundrel. He is not to be
trusted. You'd better tell Ben to be sure Jiggy pays him
for the bit and bridle right away."

"That I will," agreed Mr. Merriman. "I'll take no
promises for payment from Jiggy. His money would
be drunk up before I'd see it." Mr. Merriman glanced
at Felicity and stopped talking. But Felicity knew all

about Mr. Nye. Everyone knew he drank too much rum. When he did, he went into rages and left his work undone. His house was always a mess, and his fences were always falling down. Felicity didn't dislike him for any of those reasons. She hated Mr. Nye because he killed poor cows and horses that were too old to work anymore and made leather from their hides.

"What's Mr. Nye going to do with his new horse? He's not going to work it to death, too, is he, Father?" asked Felicity.

"Don't you worry about Jiggy Nye's new horse," said Mr. Merriman. "I'm sure it's strong and healthy. Jiggy Nye would be foolish to mistreat it." He kissed Felicity on the forehead. "Now you run along home. Your mother will be wondering what's become of you and that ginger. Good-bye, my child."

"Good-bye, Father. Good day, Mrs. Fitchett," said Felicity.

"Farewell, Miss Felicity," said Mrs. Fitchett.

Felicity stepped out into the bright afternoon. She walked home thinking only one thing. *Mr. Nye has a new horse, and I'm going to see it—somehow—as soon as I can.*

Penny

*L*ate afternoon sunshine slanted through the window onto Felicity's back. Felicity squirmed. She had a terrible itch and didn't know how to scratch it. She couldn't reach it with her left hand. Her right hand was inky, because she was practicing her script. She jiggled her shoulders up and down. She held her breath and rubbed her sides with her elbows. She leaned back and wiggled her shoulder against the chair.

"Felicity, my dear!" exclaimed her mother. "Why are you twitching and fidgeting so?"

"I have the most awful itch, Mother," said Felicity. "I think my stays are laced too tight today. They're so pinching and uncomfortable." Felicity pulled at her stays, which were laced up her back like a tight vest.

Mrs. Merriman shook her head and laughed. "You

think your stays are laced too tight every day! But you do grow so fast, maybe you are right. Come here, my child, and I will loosen them for you."

"Thank you, Mother," said Felicity. She sighed with relief as her mother loosened the laces.

"I've told you many times, Lissie. Your stays will not pinch you if you sit up straight," said Mrs. Merriman. "And they will not be uncomfortable if you move gracefully instead of galloping about." She straightened Felicity's cap. "There, now, pretty one. You are set to rights. Fetch me your paper, so that I may see your handwriting practice."

Felicity blushed as she handed her mother the paper. "I haven't quite finished it, Mother," she said.

"So I see," said Mrs. Merriman. "The first few letters are very fine. But you lost patience when you got to the letter H. The rest of the letters go trip-trotting all over the page and then turn into sketches of horses!" She put the paper down and looked Felicity in the eye. "Lissie, what am I to do with you? You must learn to finish what you begin. If you spent half as much time on your letters as you do daydreaming of horses, you'd have the finest hand in Williamsburg." She sighed. "Go along to the well now. Fetch some water and scrub your hand. Mind you get the ink off."

"Yes, Mother," said Felicity. She turned to go, but stopped at the door. "Mother," she asked. "May I help Ben make a delivery?"

"Yes, my lively girl," laughed her mother. "I know very well there's no use trying to keep you inside when your mind is already out and away."

"Thank you, Mother!" said Felicity as she flew out the door.

"Lissie! Your hat!" called her mother. But she was too late. Felicity was already halfway to the well.

—❧✿❧—

Felicity's hand was still a little wet and a little inky when she rushed down the street to her father's store. Just as she got there, she saw Ben come out. He stopped and looked up the street toward the silversmith's shop, then down the street toward the church, as if he were not sure which way to go.

"Ben, do you know the way to Mrs. Fitchett's house?" Felicity asked.

Ben shrugged. "I'll find it."

Ben's shyness didn't stop Felicity. "Come on," she said. "I'll show you."

Ben shrugged again. "As you wish," he said. Then he was quiet.

Felicity didn't mind. It was so lovely to be outside. And this was just the kind of afternoon she loved best. She could see a few leaves that had turned bright gold. They were like small banners announcing that summer's heat was ending and fall's cool weather was on its way.

Felicity was supposed to be leading Ben, but Ben took such long strides Felicity had to trot to keep up with him. Finally she lifted the hems of her petticoats so that she could take long strides, too. It felt wonderful to be able to stretch her legs.

"Oh, I wish I could wear breeches," she said.

"What?" asked Ben.

"Breeches," said Felicity. "Gowns and petticoats are so bothersome. I'm forever stepping on my hem and tripping unless I take little baby steps. Small steps are supposed to look ladylike. But I can't get anywhere. 'Tis a terrible bother. In breeches your legs are free. You can straddle horses, jump over fences, run as fast as you wish. You can do anything."

Ben didn't answer, but he shifted the sack of oats to his other shoulder. Now Felicity could see his face.

"It's very tiresome to be a girl sometimes," Felicity went on. "There are so many things a young lady must not do. I'm told the same things over and over again. Don't talk too loud. Don't walk too fast. Don't fidget. Don't dirty your hands. Don't be impatient." Felicity sighed. "It's very hard. You're lucky to be a lad. You can do whatever you like."

Ben shook his head. "I *can't* do whatever I like. I'm an apprentice."

"Oh," said Felicity. They walked in silence for a while. Then Felicity asked, "Are you happy here in Williamsburg?"

"Happy enough," said Ben.

"I imagine you miss your family and friends back in Yorktown," said Felicity. "And I'm sure they miss you, too. If I loved someone, I could never let him go away from me. I would be too miserable and lonely." She glanced over at Ben. Maybe he was lonely. "You'll be happier here when you have some friends," she said.

"Aye," said Ben. Then he hid his face behind the

sack of oats amd was quiet again.

Felicity and Ben made their way along the dusty,
wide main street of Williamsburg. It was not very
busy this afternoon. The city was just beginning to
wake up after the hot, sleepy summer. Mrs. Vobe was
welcoming some guests to her tavern. The milliner had
opened the windows of her shop to catch the first fall
breezes. Here and there, peeking out from behind a
hedge or a fence, Felicity saw yellow flowers nodding
their heads to welcome autumn.

After they delivered the oats to Mrs. Fitchett's
stable, Ben said, "I can find my way to the tannery and
home from here."

Felicity kept right on walking. "Mr. Nye has a new
horse, and I've a curiosity to see it," she said. Felicity
half expected Ben to tell her to run along home, but
he didn't say anything. *Sometimes I'm glad he's so quiet,*
thought Felicity. She grinned to herself.

Jiggy Nye's tannery was on the far edge of the town,
out where the neat fenced yards grew ragged and pas-
tures stretched off into the woods. Felicity could smell
the tannery vats before she could see the tumbledown
tannery shed. The vats were huge kettles full of yellow-

brown ooze made of foul-smelling fish oil or sour beer.
Mr. Nye soaked animal hides in them to make leather.

"Whoosh!" said Felicity. "The smell of the tannery is
enough to make your hair curl!"

"Aye!" said Ben. "The whole business stinks."

Suddenly they heard angry shouts and a horse's
frightened whinnies.

"Down, ye hateful beast! Down, ye savage!" they
heard Mr. Nye yell.

Felicity ran to the pasture gate. She saw Mr. Nye in
the pasture, trying to back a horse between the shafts of
a work cart. The horse was rearing up and whinnying.
It jerked its head and pawed the air with its hooves.
Mr. Nye was shouting and pulling on a rope that was
tied around the horse's neck.

"I'll beat ye down, I will," yelled Mr. Nye.

Ben caught up with Felicity and pulled her arm.
"Stay back," he ordered.

"No! I want to see the horse," said Felicity. She
stood behind the open gate and stared. The horse was
wild-eyed and skinny. Its coat was rough and matted
with dirt. Its mane and tail were knotted with burrs.
But Felicity could see that it was a fine animal with

long, strong legs and a proud, arched neck. "Oh, 'tis a beautiful horse," whispered Felicity. "Beautiful."

Mr. Nye and the horse both seemed to hear her at the same moment. The horse calmed and turned toward Felicity. That gave Mr. Nye a chance to tighten the rope around its neck. When the horse felt the rope, it went wild again. Mr. Nye was nearly pulled off the ground when it reared up on its hind legs.

"Ye beast!" Mr. Nye shouted. He glared at Ben and barked, "Help me! Get in here and grab this rope!"

Ben darted into the pen and grabbed the rope with Mr. Nye, but the horse reared and pawed the air more wildly than before.

"I'll beat the fire out of ye!" shouted Mr. Nye in a rage. He raised his whip to strike the horse.

"No!" cried Felicity. At that, the horse took off across the pasture, dragging Ben and Mr. Nye through the dust. They had to let go of the rope and give up.

Mr. Nye waved his arms and yelled at Felicity, "Get away with ye! You've spooked my horse, ye bothersome chit of a girl."

Felicity called out, "You spooked the horse yourself. You know you did!"

"Arrgh!" Mr. Nye snarled. He turned his red-rimmed eyes on Ben and growled, "What are ye doing here?"

"I've brought the bit and bridle you ordered from Master Merriman," Ben said.

Mr. Nye held out his hand. "Give it here."

Ben stepped back. "I'm to wait for payment," he said.

"Get away with ye!" shouted Mr. Nye. "Keep your blasted bit. That horse won't take the bit no matter. Go now, before I take my whip to the two of ye. Hear me?"

Ben turned to go, but Felicity backed away slowly. She couldn't stop watching the beautiful horse. It was running back and forth across the pasture, trapped inside the fence.

"Felicity, come along!" said Ben.

Felicity turned and followed Ben, but she did not even see the road in front of her. "Isn't she beautiful, Ben?" Felicity said. "Isn't she a dream of a horse?"

"Aye," agreed Ben. "She's a chestnut mare, a blood horse."

"That means she's a thoroughbred, doesn't it?" said Felicity.

"Aye. It means she was trained to be a gentleman's mount," said Ben. "That horse is not bred to drag a work cart."

"She was never meant to belong to the likes of Mr. Nye!" Felicity exclaimed. "She's much too fine! Oh, just once I'd love to ride a horse like that!"

"She'd be too fast for you," said Ben. "You'd never stay on her." He shook his head grimly. "Besides, that horse won't trust anyone after the way Mr. Nye is treating her. She won't let anyone on her back ever again. That horse has gone vicious."

Felicity heard what Ben said, but she didn't believe it. She'd seen the look of frantic anger in the horse's eyes. But Felicity had seen something else, too. Under the wildness there was spirit, not viciousness. Just as under the mud and burrs there was a beautiful reddish-gold coat, as bright as a new copper penny. "Penny," whispered Felicity.

"What?" asked Ben.

"Penny," said Felicity. "That's what I'm going to call that horse. She's the color of a new copper penny. It's a good name for her, isn't it?"

"Aye," said Ben. "Because she's an independent-minded horse, that's for certain. Call her Penny for her inde*pen*dence, too."

Felicity smiled. From then on, she thought of the horse as Penny—beautiful, independent, bright, shining Penny.

By the time Felicity and Ben walked to the middle of town, the sun was melting on the horizon. They hurried along to the Merrimans' house.

"Felicity Merriman!" exclaimed her mother. "Wherever have you been all this time?"

"Ben and I stopped out at the tannery," said Felicity. "And, oh, Mother! We saw the most beautiful horse!"

"A horse?" asked Mrs. Merriman.

Mr. Merriman said, "It's Jiggy Nye's new horse, I wager."

Ben handed him the harness and bit. "Mr. Nye didn't buy these things, sir. He can't control the horse enough to harness it. 'Tis a headstrong, independent-minded horse, a bright chestnut mare, and fast as fire."

"How did Jiggy Nye come to have such a horse?" asked Mrs. Merriman.

"No one knows for sure," said Ben. "Mr. Nye says he won the horse in a bet from a man who found it straying in the woods. He says the man put a notice in the newspaper. The notice said that whoever lost the horse should come to claim it, but no one ever came. That's just Mr. Nye's story, though. It's hard to trust his word."

Felicity had never heard Ben talk so much. She was surprised at all he knew.

"It's a pity Jiggy's got hold of the horse," Mr. Merriman said. He shook his head. "It will not end well, I fear."

Felicity could tell by the look on her father's face that Penny was in danger. She made up her mind to go back to the tannery and see Penny as soon as she could.

Jiggy Nye's Threat

September begins the season of thunderstorms in Virginia. For the next three days the sky was as gray as pewter, rain fell in sheets, and the wind roared around the corners of the house. Felicity felt as trapped as Penny was in Mr. Nye's pasture. "May I go out of doors, Mother?" she asked.

"In this storm?" her mother said. "Don't be a goose! The streets are all mud, and you'll be soaked to the skin in this rain. You will just have to wait till it stops."

Felicity sighed.

"Lissie, my love," said her mother. Her gentle voice sounded tired. "Look at this apron you sewed. I've had to rip out the hem on it again. It's supposed to be twenty stitches to the inch, Lissie. And in a line. Yours fly all over. Your sister Nan sews more carefully, and she is but six years old."

"I'm sorry, Mother. Indeed I am," said Felicity. "My hands just won't go so slow."

Mrs. Merriman patted Felicity's hands and gave her the apron. "You will have to teach your hands to slow down, my girl," she said.

Felicity held up the apron and shook her head sadly. "All these miles and miles of stitches! They are never finished," she said.

"Slow and steady, my child," said her mother. "They'll be done faster if you do them right, so that you don't have to sew every seam twice. Remember, haste makes waste."

"Haste makes waste," Felicity repeated. She and her mother had to smile at each other, for Felicity was told that haste makes waste at least once every day of her life.

Felicity settled down to her stitching and tried very hard to be careful—for a little while. At last, the sun broke through the clouds, and Felicity was allowed to go outside.

"Take these preserves to Mrs. Deare," said her

mother. "Nan and William will go with you. They've been cooped up, too."

Felicity hid her disappointment. She wanted to go see Penny by herself. She didn't want her little sister and brother dragging along. They were so slow! And she was so eager to see Penny. But she had no choice.

William toddled along on his fat little legs, dragging a stick through the mud. He stopped to pick up stones and drop them in puddles. He seemed to be trying to get as much mud on his shoes as he could. Nan walked in little ladylike steps, picking her way carefully around the puddles. Felicity was forever having to turn around and wait for careful Nan and muddy William.

"Oooh, Lissie," said Nan. "Look at the fine hat in the milliner's window! It has a whole bouquet of flowers on it! Let's go in and look at it."

"No! Come along, Nan," said Felicity. "I don't want to waste time with that foolishness."

Nan was miffed for a while, but she put on her sweetest face when they reached Mrs. Deare's house. Mrs. Deare gave Nan and William each a cake. She fussed over them until Felicity thought she'd burst with impatience. Then, when they were at last on their way to the tannery, Nan announced, "I want to go home. I won't go any farther."

"Nan!" Felicity said sternly. "We're going to the tannery. Come along."

"No!" said Nan, sticking out her lip. "The tannery smells terrible. I won't go."

"I won't, too," said William.

Felicity had an idea. "Nan," she said slowly. "There are lots of flowers out by the tannery. You can pick them and put them in your hat, so it will look just like the one in the milliner's window. Won't that be fine?"

"Well, perhaps," said Nan. "But I won't speak to that dirty old Mr. Nye. He's bad."

"Bad," repeated William. He swung his sticks as if they were swords.

Felicity led them along past Mr. Nye's house to the pasture. And there was Penny! She was thinner, and her coat was even more matted and dirty. There was a red cut on one leg, as if she had hurt it trying to jump over the fence. Mr. Nye had tied Penny to a stake. The poor horse was straining at the rope, pawing the ground, and jerking and tossing her head.

"Horse!" said William.

"Her name is Penny," said Felicity, "because she's the color of a penny and because she's so inde*pen*dent."

"What does 'independent' mean?" asked Nan.

"It means she has a free spirit," said Felicity. "Penny wants to run." Felicity climbed up on the pasture fence.

"Don't go near her!" warned Nan.

"She won't hurt me. She will never hurt me," said Felicity. She called to Penny softly, slowly, "Penny! Penny, love. Look here. Look what I've brought you." Felicity tossed a lump of sugar close to Penny's nose.

"So much sugar, Lissie!" said Nan. "Where did you get it?"

"Hush!" said Felicity. She didn't take her eyes off Penny. "And don't tell about it when we get home, or—"

"So!" Mr. Nye's voice croaked in her ear. Felicity's heart stopped. Mr. Nye grabbed her by the shoulders and pulled her down off the fence. Nan knelt next to William and held him tight.

"You're that sly red-headed chit, ain't ye?" said Mr. Nye. "Didn't I tell ye to stay away from my horse?"

Felicity yanked herself out of his grasp. "I'm not hurting her," she said.

"This horse is none of your business, hear me?" growled Mr. Nye. "She's a vicious animal. She knocked the fence down trying to jump out of the pasture. I had to tie her up. I don't want ye spookin' her. Stay away!"

Felicity was frightened, but she was angry. "You are the one who scares the poor horse," she said to Mr. Nye. "You have no right to treat her so badly."

Mr. Nye grabbed Felicity again, but just then Penny whinnied wildly.

"Quiet, ye nag!" Mr. Nye shouted at Penny. He picked up a big stick and climbed into the pasture. As he came near, Penny reared. With a mighty pull, she broke the rope that tied her. Mr. Nye lost his balance and fell back into the dirt. He shook his fist at Penny as she ran away to the far end of the pasture.

"Ye worthless nag!" Mr. Nye yelled after Penny. His face was spattered with mud. "I'd give ye to anyone who can ride ye! *Anyone* can have ye! Hear me?" Mr. Nye stomped toward his house. Suddenly he turned toward Felicity and snarled, "And you! Get yourself and those brats out of here! I'll skin ye alive if I see ye here again." Then he stormed off.

Nan was crying. "Let's go! Please, let's go," she begged. She pulled on Felicity's petticoats and dragged her away. Felicity looked back to see Penny galloping around the pasture. At least Penny was not tied to the stake anymore. She was fenced in, but she could run and move. *Good for you, Penny*, thought Felicity. *Don't you let Mr. Nye scare you. I won't let him scare me!*

At suppertime, it was William who gave it away. "Big horse," he said. "Bad man." He waved his spoon wildly.

"Shh," hissed Nan.

"What's all this?" asked Mother. "You've not been out to see that horse of Jiggy Nye's, have you?"

"Felicity made us go," said Nan. "And the horse made Mr. Nye fall down in the mud. Then Mr. Nye called the horse a nag, and he said anyone could take it if they could ride it. And he said he would skin us alive if we ever came back!"

"Hush, my child!" scolded Mrs. Merriman. "It's not proper to repeat such talk." She looked at Felicity, and her face was serious. "Jiggy Nye told you not to come back, and you won't—ever. His tannery is not a place for children."

"He was going to strike the horse with a big stick!" added Nan.

"The man's a villain of the worst sort," muttered Mr. Merriman. "A horse beater."

Ben spoke up. "He'll kill the horse, sir," he said. "Mark me, he will."

"Oh, Father," cried Felicity. "We can't let Mr. Nye hurt Penny! We've got to help her. We've got to get her away from Mr. Nye! Can't we buy her?"

"Gracious, no!" exclaimed her mother. "We've Old Bess for your father to ride, and Blossom to draw the cart."

"Bess is so slow, it's faster if you walk yourself!" said Felicity.

"Young lady," said Mrs. Merriman. "It would not harm you to go more slowly in all things—stitches and speeches and thinking, too."

Mr. Merriman spoke gently. "We've no need for a troublesome horse like that, my child. It would be useless to us, too. No one wants a horse that cannot be

ridden. Besides, Marcus has enough to do with Old
Bess and Blossom. He does not have time to care for
another horse."

"But I would take care of her," said Felicity eagerly.
"I would tame her and teach her. I would do everything."

Ben looked up.

Mrs. Merriman sighed. "Lissie," she said. "My
impatient, headstrong Lissie. You have not the patience
to sew a seam properly. You leave your writing practice
half done. You lead your sister and brother to dangerous places and never stop to think. A willful girl and a
willful horse is more than one family can handle. You
must put that horse out of your head. Do you hear me?"

"Yes, ma'am," Felicity answered. For it was true,
she did hear what her mother said. But she did not put
the horse out of her head or her heart.

Ben's Promise

he last sliver of moonlight made a silvery path across the floor of Felicity's room. As sound-lessly as in a dream, Felicity edged out of bed. She slipped her petticoats over her shift, pulled on her stockings and garters, and tiptoed to the door. Down the stairs she crept, skipping the step that creaked. She was shaking with nervousness.

It was better when she was outside. Felicity put on her shoes. Then she gathered her petticoats in her hand and ran fast through the garden, through the dark streets, past the sleeping houses. On she ran to the edge of town, where the trees grew close to the road and she was just another ghostly shadow.

By the time Felicity reached the pasture, she was out of breath. She stood on the lowest rail of the fence and searched the darkness for Penny. The horse was tied to a stake by a thick rope. Penny looked up and tossed her head.

Felicity did not dare speak aloud. "I'm here. It's me," she whispered to Penny. "You don't have to trust me yet. But you will. I know you will."

Penny did not move. Felicity left a small apple near the stake. "Good-bye," she whispered. Then she ran home. The sky was only just beginning to grow light around the edges.

When Felicity came to breakfast, her mother looked at her. "Felicity!" she said. "Your petticoats are wet and muddy. Most likely your stockings are wet, too, all the way up to your garters. What on earth have you been doing?"

Felicity looked down at her muddy hem.

"I was just . . . just in the garden."

Mrs. Merriman smiled. "Digging around the pump-kins you planted?" she asked. "My impatient one! They'll not grow faster just to please you. Now sit down and eat your breakfast."

I need breeches, thought Felicity. *Then I can run freely. Then it won't matter if I get wet and muddy. But how can I get them?*

She found the answer in the mending pile. It was a pair of Ben's breeches made of thin black cotton. Felicity knew Ben didn't wear these breeches very often, just to church sometimes. He wouldn't miss them if she borrowed them for a while.

The next morning before dawn, Felicity sneaked out of the house again. This time, she stopped by the stable. She had hidden Ben's breeches there, under an old bucket. She put the breeches on over her shift and tied them around her waist with a rope. Ben was skinny but tall, so the breeches went down to Felicity's ankles. As she ran through the silent streets toward the tannery, her legs felt so free! For once she could run as fast as she wanted to, without petticoats to hold her back.

Morning after morning, before anyone was awake, Felicity slipped out of the house to visit Penny. At first, Felicity stayed outside the pasture. After a few days, she sat on the top rail of the fence. She sat near, but not *too* near, the stake to which Penny was tied. Felicity never spoke aloud. She knew that if she were rough or noisy, she would frighten the horse. Even though Felicity couldn't sit still for her stitchery, she could sit almost without moving at all when she was near Penny.

She felt peaceful, sitting on the rail fence those misty gray mornings, watching the beautiful horse. Sometimes Penny was calm. Sometimes she pulled on her rope or raised her head to sniff the wind. *She's thinking about running away*, thought Felicity. *She's thinking about freedom.*

The first time Felicity climbed off the fence into the pasture, Penny tossed her head and danced about. But she did not whinny or shy away. Soon Felicity thought Penny expected her to come each morning and maybe even looked forward to seeing her. Penny knew Felicity was kind and patient and would not hurt her. With all her heart, Felicity wished she had more time to spend with Penny so that the horse would trust her completely.

One morning after breakfast, Felicity was trying to hide her yawns as she practiced her stitches. She sat up straight when she heard her mother ask, "Ben, did you put your breeches in the mending pile, as I told you to?"

"Yes, ma'am," answered Ben.

"I don't see them there," said Mrs. Merriman. "Where are they?"

"I do not know, ma'am," said Ben.

"Well, look about you, lad!" said Mrs. Merriman. "Breeches don't just disappear!"

"Yes, ma'am," said Ben.

Felicity kept her head down but watched Ben out of the corner of her eye. He looked confused and a little embarrassed. *He has no idea what has happened to his breeches,* thought Felicity. *I wonder how he would feel if he did know?*

But no one knew Felicity's secret. No one knew about the lovely times she had with Penny all those dreamlike mornings. Felicity's secret made her happy. All day long, while she was mending or practicing her writing or playing with Nan and William, Felicity thought about Penny. The beautiful horse was growing more friendly every day.

Felicity always took an apple to Penny. One morning, after Felicity had been visiting her for a few weeks, Penny took the apple right from her hand. Felicity held her breath when she felt Penny's warm nose tickling her fingers. She stood still. She did not try to touch Penny. From that time on, Penny made a game of asking for the apple. She would nudge Felicity gently and nicker until Felicity held the apple out to her.

On one drizzly morning, Penny nuzzled Felicity for the apple as usual. But before she took it, Penny raised her head, whinnied, and seemed worried. Felicity stepped back.

"What's wrong, Penny?" she whispered. Just then Felicity heard dogs barking and yowling. Mr. Nye! He was coming out to the pasture! Felicity dropped to the ground, rolled under the fence, and hid in the tall, scraggly grass. Penny whinnied and pawed the ground.

"Don't start with me, ye useless horse!" Mr. Nye snarled. He came into the pasture and stood by the fence, near Felicity's hiding spot. Felicity dared not move. Her heart thumped as she watched Mr. Nye put a bucket of water on the ground in front of Penny. "No oats till ye let me ride ye," he muttered to the horse. "Starve to death for all I care." As soon as Mr. Nye turned his back, Felicity got up and ran home as fast as she could.

But nothing—not even Mr. Nye—could keep Felicity away from Penny. The mornings grew more chill as September blew into October. Felicity shivered when she pulled herself out of bed these mornings. But the sky stayed dark longer, so she had more time with Penny.

There was frost on the grass the morning Felicity untied Penny's rope from the stake and led her around the pasture for the first time. Penny followed behind Felicity, leaving the whole length of the rope between them. But after a week or so, Penny followed with her nose right next to Felicity's shoulder. Sometimes Penny even pushed at her playfully. At the end of their walks, Penny let Felicity stroke her neck and rub her nose.

"Aye, that's my girl," Felicity whispered in her ear. "You know I love you, don't you, Penny? Don't you, girl? You know I won't rush you."

The day came when all Felicity's patience was rewarded. One morning Penny was standing quietly next to the fence as if she were waiting for Felicity. Slowly, Felicity untied the rope from the stake.

Slowly, she climbed onto Penny's back. At first, Penny trotted. Felicity sat up straight and held on to her mane. As Penny's stiff trot eased into a smooth canter, Felicity leaned closer and closer to Penny's neck. Soon they were flying across the pasture, moving as swift and sure as the wind. Penny's hooves hardly seemed to touch the ground. Above them, the sky was pearly gray. The wind made Felicity's eyes water. She had moved that fast only in her dreams.

Every day Penny did something new. The first time Penny jumped over a small pile of hay, Felicity was so surprised she fell off the horse's back. After that, they tried higher and higher jumps—a heap of rocks, a tree stump, a stack of logs. Felicity never fell off again. She learned that Penny tensed her neck just before she jumped. That was a signal to Felicity to hold on tight.

Penny was full of surprises. One morning, she carried Felicity across the pasture in a gallop, then leaped effortlessly over the broken-down part of the fence. That morning they rode farther than ever before. Felicity lost track of time as they cantered deeper and deeper into the woods with no fences to stop them. When they jumped back over the fence, back into the pasture, Felicity retied Penny's rope to the stake quickly. She knew it was late. The sky was turning pink, and the mist was lifting out of the meadows.

Felicity ran home. She slipped into the stable as usual and changed from the breeches to her petticoats quickly. She was just rolling up the breeches to hide

them under the bucket when she heard someone say,
"You!"

It was Ben.

Felicity froze with the breeches in her hands.

She said nothing.

"What do you have there?" asked Ben in his coldest voice. He came forward. "What? *You* have my best Sunday breeches?" He took them out of Felicity's hands and looked at them. "They're wet and covered with mud!"

He sniffed them. "Whoosh! They smell like a horse!" He looked at Felicity. "Felicity, are you—"

Felicity interrupted him. "I'm sorry, Ben. I was borrowing them. I just . . . I just needed them."

Ben sat down. "Felicity, tell me what you are doing," he said quietly.

Felicity took a deep breath. "I'm visiting Penny—the horse at the tannery."

"That horse?" said Ben. His eyes were wide.

"Oh, she's so fine, Ben," said Felicity. "She's gentle and dear. And she's so fast!"

"What!" Ben exclaimed. "You mean you're riding her?"

"Oh, yes!" said Felicity. "It's a wonder, Ben. It's just like riding the wind."

Ben shook his head. "Felicity, I don't know whether you are the bravest or the most foolish girl I've ever known," he said. "I'd be afraid to ride that horse. She looks like she would throw any rider sky-high!"

"She was afraid at first, but now she trusts me," said Felicity.

"How long have you been going out there?" Ben asked.

"Every day since the rain stopped," Felicity answered.

"That's almost one month!" Ben said. "You've been up before dawn, dressing in my breeches, and running out to see that horse for one month?"

"Yes."

Ben sat still. He stared at Felicity and said nothing. Then he asked, "How long can you keep doing this? You can't do it forever. Mr. Nye will surely see you someday. And Penny *is* his horse."

"I heard Mr. Nye say that anyone who could ride her could have her," said Felicity. "I can ride her. So she will be mine."

Ben sighed. "Felicity, you set your heart on things too much. I don't believe Mr. Nye or your father will let you keep that horse." He saw Felicity's stubborn frown, and he grinned. "But then I never would have believed you could have ridden that horse, either."

"I am going to get Penny away from Mr. Nye somehow," Felicity said. "I have to."

"Aye," said Ben. "You'd best do it soon."

"I can't hurry Penny," said Felicity. "I have to be patient with her."

Ben nodded.

"So, then," asked Felicity, "do you want your breeches back?"

"Not smelling the way they do!" laughed Ben. "No, you need them more than I do. You keep them as long as you like. I'll keep your secret."

"Thank you, Ben," said Felicity. She gave him a quick grin and hurried in to breakfast.

Sharing Felicity's secret seemed to change Ben. He wasn't so shy. Sometimes he whistled, and he even surprised everyone by joking once or twice at supper.

And he was true to his word.

That Sunday, Mrs. Merriman said, "Ben, have you still not found your good breeches? They were fine, expensive India cotton. 'Tis not like you to be so careless."

"I beg your pardon, ma'am," said Ben. "I know where they are now."

Felicity felt her face growing red. Was Ben going to tell?

"I lent them to a friend," said Ben easily.

"Indeed!" said Mrs. Merriman. "May I ask why?"

"My friend needs them more than I do," said Ben.

"Well," sighed Mrs. Merriman. "Dust off your old woolen breeches then. We needn't go to church looking like a band of ruffians."

Felicity smiled at Ben. He had called her his friend. He truly *was* a friend to her.

All that week, Felicity thought long and hard about what Ben had said. She knew he was right. She couldn't keep her secret much longer.

Independence

Felicity brushed Penny until she was as shining as the sun. She combed the horse's mane and untangled the knots in her tail. Mr. Nye never brushed Penny, and usually Felicity was afraid to do more than pull the burrs off her coat. She did not want Mr. Nye to know someone was caring for Penny. But today was different. Today the secret would end.

Penny knew something was happening. She stood very still and let Felicity brush her.

"There, Penny, my beauty," Felicity said at last. "No one would recognize you. You're so clean and beautiful and so peaceful and calm."

Penny nudged her affectionately. Felicity rubbed Penny's nose. "I love you, Penny," she said. "Are you ready?"

Penny stood next to the pasture fence and let

Felicity climb on her back. Felicity wore her coral necklace for good luck. She wore her favorite gown, too, so that she and Penny would both look their best. "We're off, girl," Felicity said to Penny. "Now don't you worry. Everything will be fine."

The sun was rising, tinting the rooftops gold, as Felicity rode down the main street. The few people who were up stared and wondered. Was that the Merriman girl, riding astride a horse? And what a horse it was! A beauty! Where did such a horse come from?

Nan was carrying the breakfast bread from the kitchen to the house when Felicity rode into the yard. Nan's mouth fell open in astonishment. She called out, "Mother! Father! Come quick!"

"What's all the fuss and bother?" Mr. Merriman asked. He came outside wiping his face with a napkin. He stopped still when he saw Felicity riding Penny.

"Look!" cried William behind him. "Lissie's horse! Lissie's horse!"

"Felicity Merriman!" exclaimed Mother. "What are you doing? Where did you get that horse?"

"It's Penny," said Felicity. "It's the horse I told you about."

Ben came toward her. Penny stepped back nervously. "It's all right, Penny," said Felicity. "It's all right." She stroked the horse's neck, and Penny calmed down. Slowly, Ben reached up and touched Penny's neck.

"Is that the horse from Jiggy Nye's tannery?" asked Mr. Merriman. "What on earth are you doing with Jiggy Nye's horse? Does he know you have it? Why have you brought her here?"

"I wanted you to see her, Father," said Felicity quickly. "I wanted to show you how lovely and gentle she is. Penny was never vicious. It was only that Mr. Nye beat her and hurt her. She did not trust him— or anyone. She wouldn't let me ride her for the longest time."

"The longest time?" asked Mrs. Merriman. "Whatever do you mean? How long have you been . . . been going to her?"

"Near five weeks now," said Felicity. "Every morning."

Mrs. Merriman sank down on the step. "Five weeks? And we never knew!"

"But how did you tame her?" asked Mr. Merriman. "Who showed you what to do?"

"Penny herself. She showed me what to do," said Felicity. "All I had to do was to be patient and careful. I had to wait for her to trust me."

"She's a beautiful horse," said Mr. Merriman. "And she seems as mild as a lamb. But she is not your horse to ride, even if you did tame her. You know it is wrong to borrow a horse without asking. You must take her back to the tannery now. You must apologize to Jiggy Nye for riding his horse. And you must never ride Penny again unless Jiggy Nye says that you may."

"But Father, you don't understand! I want to keep her!" cried Felicity. "I heard Mr. Nye say that anyone who could ride her could have her. I can ride her, so she's mine."

Mr. Merriman shook his head. "Lissie, Lissie," he said. "It is you who misunderstood. No one would give away a horse like this. She belongs to Jiggy Nye. You must return her."

"But he beats the horse and starves her," said Ben.

"That may be true, but it is still his horse," said Mr. Merriman firmly.

"Can't we buy her, Father?" begged Felicity. "Can't we keep her? Can't Penny stay?"

But Father had no time to answer. For at that moment, Jiggy Nye came reeling into the yard. Penny reared, and Felicity had to grab on to her mane to stay on her back. Nan shrieked and William wailed.

"I found ye!" yelled Mr. Nye. "Ye headstrong chit of a girl! You've stolen my horse! Get down off my horse!"

Felicity leaned down and threw her arms around Penny's neck. Penny was trembling. "You said anyone who could ride her could have her," Felicity said to Mr. Nye.

"I never did!" snarled Mr. Nye.

Nan cried out, "You did! You did! I heard you, you bad old man!"

Mr. Nye shouted, "I never meant no girl could steal that horse from me!"

"No one is trying to steal your horse," Mr. Merriman said. "My daughter misunderstood. She was wrong to take your horse, but it was a child's honest mistake. I make my apologies for her."

"Mistake!" said Mr. Nye. "Taking a horse is a crime!"

"The only crime here is the way you mistreat this horse," said Mr. Merriman. "You don't deserve to own

Penny. I would buy her from you—"

"Hah!" shouted Mr. Nye. "Never! I will never sell this horse to you and your bold-faced daughter. The horse is mine, and it always will be mine. I can treat it any way I want to. Hear me? Now tell your brat to get off my horse before I rip her down myself!" he ordered.

"No!" cried Felicity. "Don't let him take Penny! Father, please don't!"

Mr. Merriman looked up at Felicity sadly. "Penny does not belong to you, Felicity. You must let Jiggy Nye take her."

Felicity held Penny tight. "Please, Father, please," she begged. "We can't let Penny go."

Mr. Merriman gently opened Felicity's arms and slid her off Penny's back.

Mr. Nye put a rope around Penny's neck and pulled it tight. He turned to Felicity and said, "Don't you come sneaking around! If I see you near this horse, I swear I'll kill it! I'll tan its hide before I let you touch it again."

Mr. Merriman put both his hands on Felicity's shoulders. "I'll not have you speak so roughly to my daughter, Nye. Be off with you!" he said.

Mr. Nye spat in the dust. Then he yanked on the rope and led Penny away.

Felicity felt dead inside. Penny was gone, and all her hopes were gone, too. "Penny!" she whispered. Then she turned and ran to the stable so that no one could hear her cry.

A while later, Father came into the stable to find her. Felicity was stroking Old Bess. She took comfort in Bess's warm, horsey smell.

Father put his arm around Felicity. "Have you cried all your tears, my child?" he asked.

Felicity nodded. They sat quietly for a while. Then Felicity said, "It was all a waste, wasn't it? It was all for nothing."

"Nothing?" said her father. "Didn't you tame that horse? Didn't I see you riding her, looking as fine as a queen?"

"But look how it ended," said Felicity. "Mr. Nye has taken Penny back. I was wrong to ride off with her, and wrong to think that I could keep her. I was wrong to try to make her mine."

"No, Felicity, my dear," said Father. "It is never

wrong to try to earn something you love. Indeed, 'tis only wrong not to try. You hoped for something and you put hard work behind your hope. I can only be proud of a daughter who can do that." He kissed Felicity's forehead. "You come back to the house when you're ready."

After Father left, Felicity pulled Ben's breeches out from under the bucket. She went to Ben's room and knocked. When he opened the door, Felicity held out his breeches. She said nothing.

Ben took the breeches. Suddenly he said, "Felicity, I have a little money. Maybe if we offered Mr. Nye money . . ."

"No, Ben," said Felicity. "You heard him say he will never sell Penny to us. He's too hateful."

"But Penny will never let Mr. Nye ride her," said Ben. "If he touches her, she'll go vicious again. Then he will beat her, and starve her, and soon I fear he'll—"

"He'll kill her, Ben," said Felicity.

"Aye," whispered Ben. "I fear he will."

"We've got to save her somehow," said Felicity. "We've got to. What can we do?"

"If only you could hide her somewhere," murmured Ben.

"Penny's not a horse that was meant to live hidden away," said Felicity. "She'd die of sadness if she were kept closed up in a stable or a pen."

"You are right," nodded Ben. "She'd be better off loose again, running free in the woods."

Felicity said softly, "Aye, she'd be better off running free." Then Felicity looked at Ben. "She'd be better off running free," she said louder.

Ben looked sad. "Felicity," he said slowly. "If you let her loose, you will never see her again."

Felicity nodded.

"And if you untie her and open the pasture gate and let her go, then that would be stealing," said Ben. "The punishment for horse theft is hanging."

Felicity nodded again. Without a word, she took the breeches out of Ben's hands and left.

That night, Felicity didn't sleep at all. It was still dark, still the middle of the night when she crept out of bed, pulled on Ben's breeches, and ran along the familiar path to Penny's pasture.

The pasture gate was fastened shut with a heavy chain and lock, so Felicity climbed over the fence. She was surprised to see that Penny was not tied to the stake as she usually was. *Why didn't Mr. Nye tether her?* Felicity wondered. Felicity whistled softly, and Penny trotted over to her and nuzzled her hello. Felicity climbed onto Penny's back and whispered in her ear, "That's my girl, Penny. That's my fine one. Come on now, girl. Let's fly."

And just like all the mornings before, Penny trotted, then cantered, then galloped across the pasture. Faster and faster she flew. Felicity buried her face in Penny's mane and held on tight. Swiftly and smoothly, Penny sped across the pasture toward the tumbledown part of the fence. Felicity looked ahead and gasped in fear. The fence had been fixed! It loomed high and solid before them.

Penny can't jump that fence, Felicity thought. *It's too high.* But with one graceful leap, Penny jumped and sailed over the highest rail. And just as she did, just as she crossed the fence, Felicity let go of Penny's mane. She slipped off Penny's back and fell with a thud inside the pasture. Penny galloped on, carried by the force of her jump, running, running toward the woods. But just as she got to the edge of the trees, Penny stopped and looked back at the pasture where Felicity lay gasping for breath.

"Go on," whispered Felicity. "Go on, Penny. You are free."

Penny hesitated. She shook her mane and nickered. Then she disappeared into the woods.

"Good-bye, Penny. Good-bye, my girl," Felicity whispered. She sat on the cold ground and waited to be sure Penny was not going to come back. Felicity didn't care how late she was getting home. She didn't care if Mr. Nye found her there in the pasture. Penny was free now, and that was all that mattered.

At last Felicity stood, brushed the dirt off the breeches, and headed home. She was very weary.

Later that morning, Felicity went back to Ben's room above the stable. "Here are your breeches, Ben," she said.

Ben took the breeches. "Did you let her go?" he asked.

Felicity nodded. Her eyes filled with tears. "Penny

is free," she said. "She freed herself."

"It's the best thing," said Ben.

"Aye," said Felicity. "But I hope she doesn't feel I've abandoned her. That would break my heart. She knows that I love her, doesn't she, Ben?"

"She knows," said Ben seriously. "She knows you love her so much you let her go free. You gave her what she needed most—her independence."

Felicity was quiet. Then she said, "Aye. That's it. Her independence."

The next Sunday, as they were all setting out for church, Mrs. Merriman said, "Well, Ben! I see your friend returned those breeches at last! They're mended nicely, too."

"Yes, ma'am," said Ben.

"Mind you keep an eye on them, lad," said Mrs. Merriman.

"Yes, ma'am, I will," said Ben. "But if my friend should ever need them, I'd be honored to lend them again."

He and Felicity shared a secret smile.

Apple Butter Day

elicity sat high atop the roof of her house and tilted her face up to the sun. The rooftop was a fine place to be on a bright blue October morning like this.

Felicity leaned back against the chimney. She put one leg on either side of the steep roof. The shingles were warm against her bare legs. A restless breeze played with her petticoats. Felicity shaded her eyes with her hand and looked out over the treetops and rooftops of Williamsburg. She watched a bright red cardinal bird swoop across the sky. Felicity grinned. *How lovely it must feel to fly wherever you want to go, with nothing holding you down,* she thought.

"Lissie! Lissieeee!" she heard Nan calling her.

Felicity decided to ignore Nan. She knew what Nan wanted. Today was apple butter day. That's why

Felicity was on the roof. She was supposed to be picking apples for Mother to make into apple butter. The best apples were at the very top of the tree, where the branches hung over the roof. So Felicity had fetched a ladder, climbed up to the roof, and filled her apple sack quickly and easily. Now Nan wanted *her* turn to pick apples. She wanted Felicity to work in the hot, stuffy kitchen, stirring the pot of sticky apple mush. Felicity was not ready to go in.

Felicity pulled one of the apples out of the sack and rubbed it on her sleeve. She took a big bite. Mmmm! Felicity seemed to taste the warm summer sun, the wild rains of September, and the cool, dark, starry nights of autumn in that juicy, tart bite. Between chews, Felicity wiggled her loose tooth with her thumb. She couldn't wait for it to fall out. Ben was teaching her to whistle with her fingers in her mouth. She thought losing that tooth might help.

Felicity tried whistling. *If I whistled loud enough,* she thought, *Nan and everyone in Williamsburg would hear me. They'd see me up here on the roof, as high as a flag!* She smiled. *Wouldn't that be fine?*

"Lissie!" she heard Nan again. "Where are you?"

"I'm up here," Felicity answered. She waved to Nan from her perch.

"Lissie!" yelped Nan. She sounded scared. "Mother!" she called. "Come quick! Lissie's on the *roof*! Mother! Come and see."

"Whatever's the matter, Nan?" asked Mrs. Merriman. She rushed out of the kitchen. William toddled along behind her. "*What's* on the roof?" She looked up. When she saw Felicity, she gasped. "Oh my gracious! Lissie!" Then she said in a very stern voice, "Felicity Merriman, I will not shout for all the world to hear. Come down from that roof immediately."

"Yes, Mother," said Felicity. She slid down the roof to the ladder with a sinking feeling. *I've done something wrong-headed again*, she thought to herself. Felicity scrambled down the ladder so quickly she scraped her knee, lost her footing, and had to jump the last few feet to the ground.

When she landed, her mother felt her all over as if she might have broken bones. "Goodness, Lissie!" she said. "You gave me such a fright! Climbing way up on the roof like that! What were you thinking of?"

"Well, I . . . well, it didn't *seem* dangerous," said

Felicity. "And there were so many more apples at the
top of the tree."

"So you thought you could fetch the apples faster.
Is that it? Impatient as usual," said her mother. She put
her hands on Felicity's shoulders and said gently but
firmly, "You are near to ten years of age, Felicity. That's
old enough to know what's a danger to you. And that's
too old to be acting careless and childish."

Felicity shifted the heavy apple sack off her shoulder. "I'm sorry . . ."

"I know you are," said her mother kindly. "But I do
wish you would stop and think before you act. Sometimes you have no more sense than a giddy goose!" She
sighed. "And let us hope no one saw you on the roof
with your petticoats blowing above your knees, bare-
legged as a newborn babe. 'Tis wrong and unseemly for
a girl your age. Now put your shoes and stockings on
and come inside quick as you can. Nan will finish picking the apples."

Felicity trailed along behind her mother to the kitchen
house. Her heart was as heavy as the apple sack. The
kitchen was dark compared to outside. The air was hot
and thick. Rose, the cook, was peeling apples, slicing

them into four parts, and dropping them in a pot of water. Another big pot full of apple mush was burbling by the fire. Mrs. Merriman pointed to it.

"You stir, Lissie," she said. "Don't let the apples stick to the pot. And mind you don't scorch your petticoat by the fire."

Felicity stirred with a long wooden spoon. Round and round, again and again, she stirred the apple mush till her arms ached. It was tiresome work, and dull. Her hair stuck to her sweaty neck. Her hands were sore, and her back was stiff. As soon as one batch of apples was cooked soft, Rose took it away and put another pot on the fire. Felicity tried to hide her impatience. But after a while, she could not help asking, "Isn't that enough? Haven't we made hundreds of pounds of apple butter by now?"

"Goodness, no," said her mother. "A whole pound of apples makes only one pint of apple butter."

Pints were very small. Felicity sighed. "It seems to be a great deal of work for a little bit of butter. I don't think it's worthwhile," she said. "And once the apple butter's eaten, there's nothing to show for all the hard work. You are left with nothing at all."

Mrs. Merriman laughed. "I remember thinking just that same thing when I was your age," she said. "And 'tis true, there's nothing left that anyone can see. But I know that I've provided for my family, and that pleases me." She looked kindly at Felicity. "Caring for a family is a responsibility and a pleasure. It will be your most important task, and one that you must learn to do well. I want you to be a notable housewife when you are grown."

"Notable?" asked Felicity.

"Yes," said Mrs. Merriman. "A notable housewife runs her household smoothly, so that everyone in it is happy and healthy. Her life is private and quiet. She is content doing things for her family."

"Things nobody ever sees," said Felicity.

"Many lovely things are private and hidden," her mother agreed. She picked up one of the apples and sliced in half across its fat middle, instead of top to bottom. She held the halves up to Felicity. "Have you ever seen the flower that is hidden inside every apple?" she asked. "It's there for those who know how to find it."

Felicity grinned at her mother. There was indeed a flower inside the apple.

"My mother showed that to me when I was a girl and we made apple butter together," said Mother. "She taught me to sew and cook and plant a garden and run a household. Now I am teaching you. Someday you will teach your daughter."

"Oh, dear," said Felicity. "It seems a great deal to learn!"

"Indeed, yes," said Mrs. Merriman. "And that is not all you must know how to do. When I was just about your age, I had special lessons with my aunt. She taught me the proper way to act in polite society. She showed me how to serve tea and how to be a gracious hostess." She smiled at the memory. "How I loved those lessons with my aunt! I felt like a graceful young lady instead of a gawky little girl."

Felicity wiggled her tooth. She didn't say anything, but the lessons her mother described sounded fussy to her.

Mrs. Merriman looked at Felicity thoughtfully. "Perhaps it is time for you . . ." she began. Then she caught sight of the pot of apple mush. "Mercy!" she said. "*Stir*, Lissie! This batch is near to burning!" And she did not finish the sentence she had begun.

But a few nights later, Felicity found out what her mother had been about to say. It was after supper. Everyone was gathered in the parlor around the fire. Its warmth was welcome, for the sun set early these fall evenings, and the dusk was chilly. Felicity sat on a low stool next to Nan. She was helping Nan learn to read the Lord's Prayer printed on her hornbook.

Nan tilted the hornbook toward the firelight as she read slowly. "' . . . Thy kingdom come.'" Then she stopped. "Lissie," she asked. "Whose kingdom do we live in? God's or the King of England's?"

"Well, both, I suppose," answered Felicity. "Isn't that right, Father?"

Mr. Merriman, who was holding William on his knee and playing chess with Ben, looked over at his daughters and nodded. "Aye," he said. "We live in the colony of Virginia, which belongs to the King of England. He rules us, even though he lives far away. Virginia is part of his kingdom."

"But Virginia is part of God's kingdom, too," said Felicity. "Because the whole world, and heaven, and all the stars and everything there is belongs to God. See what it says here, in the rest of the prayer: 'Thy will be done on earth as it is in heaven.' That means God rules both heaven and earth."

"Which word says heaven?" asked Nan.

"This one right here," said Felicity. She pointed to it and read, "Heaven, H - E - A - V - E - N."

"You can read *everything*, can't you, Lissie?" asked Nan.

"Not everything," said Felicity. "Not yet. But I do love to read. I'd like to attend the college here in Williamsburg, and read Greek and Latin and philosophy and geography, just as the young gentlemen do."

"Oh, Lissie," laughed Nan. "That's silly! Girls aren't taught at the college."

Ben looked up from the chessboard and grinned. "Maybe you could pretend to be a boy," he said. "I have a pair of breeches you may borrow."

Felicity grinned back, but then she sighed. "I don't see why girls aren't educated, too."

Mrs. Merriman looked up from her stitching and spoke. "Girls *should* be educated. Not in Latin and Greek, but in the things they need to know to be accomplished young ladies." She looked at Mr. Merriman with a question in her eyes.

Mr. Merriman nodded and smiled. Then he said in a very pleased voice, "Felicity, your mother and I have decided it is time for you to begin *your* education."

Felicity sat up. "Am I to be apprenticed, Father?" she asked hopefully. Some girls were apprentices. They learned to be seamstresses, or to make hats, or even to work in shops. Felicity had always dreamed of working in her father's store.

"Goodness, no!" exclaimed her mother. "You are fortunate enough to be the daughter of Edward Merriman, one of Williamsburg's most important merchants. You are to be educated as a *gentlewoman*."

"Oh," said Felicity. She was disappointed. "What am I to learn?"

"The things my aunt taught me," Mrs. Merriman said. "You will have lessons in dancing, handwriting, fancy stitchery, the proper way to serve tea—"

"Tea?" interrupted Ben. "Lessons about serving tea?"

"Indeed, yes!" said Mrs. Merriman. "A lady's manners are judged by the way she serves tea. My mother brought her best teapot with her when she left England to come to Virginia. She used to say the king himself would feel at home at her tea table. She served tea as properly in Virginia as any lady did in London. Now Felicity must learn to serve tea properly, too."

"Tea and stitchery!" sighed Nan. "The lessons sound lovely!"

"I'm not very good at those quiet, sitting down kinds of things," said Felicity.

"Well," said Mrs. Merriman calmly. "Then you must improve yourself."

Felicity was beginning to feel trapped. She asked, "Who will be my teacher?"

"A very respectable gentlewoman named Miss Manderly," said Mr. Merriman. "She is going to give lessons to two other young ladies. They are sisters, and their family has just come here from England. Miss Manderly has kindly agreed to let you join them."

"Ooooh!" squealed Nan. "Young ladies from England! They'll probably already know the very most proper way to do everything, Lissie!"

"The young ladies from England will be learning from Miss Manderly just as Felicity will," said Mr. Merriman. "And they will surely learn that proper and polite behavior is the same in Virginia as it is in England."

Felicity sighed. She could see that these lessons were

going to be boring and tiresome. *I would much rather spend my time out of doors,* she thought. *I would rather be horseback riding, or playing, or digging in my garden.* But Felicity knew she could not argue, or pout, or say she would *not* go to Miss Manderly's. That would not be respectful. Besides, Felicity was sure it would do no good at all.

"The lessons begin in three days' time," said Mrs. Merriman. "So we must set to work tomorrow to make ready your best cap and stockings and clothes."

"Aye!" agreed Mr. Merriman. He smiled at Felicity fondly. "Our pretty Lissie must look her very best. She will begin her lessons looking like the finest young lady in Virginia, and all of England, too. She will make us proud, to be sure."

Felicity smiled back weakly. She was not at all sure. She pushed against her loose tooth with her tongue until it hurt.

Loose Tooth Tea

tand still, my child," said Mrs. Merriman for the hundredth time. She and Nan were kneeling on the floor, checking to be sure the hem of Felicity's outer petticoat was even. This was the day Felicity was to begin her lessons.

"Mother," said Felicity impatiently. "How will Miss Manderly know if my hem is even or not? Why does it matter?"

Mrs. Merriman sat back on her heels and looked Felicity in the eye. "Everything has to be perfect. I won't have the two young ladies from England thinking we don't know how to dress ourselves here in the colonies," she said. "I want them to see that though we may live on the edge of the wilderness, we are just as civilized as they are." She sounded very determined.

Felicity sighed. For the past three days she had been

scrubbed and scoured. Her face had been washed with buttermilk to make the skin soft. Her nose had been rubbed with lemon juice to bleach out the freckles. Her hair had been twisted up on clay rollers and combed through with a pomade of hog's fat and cinnamon. Her clothes had been let out and taken in, taken up and let down, washed, mended, starched, and ironed till they were stiff with perfection. It was all very tiresome. Felicity wiggled her tooth. Now she could push it into her lip. It was going to fall out soon. *Not much longer,* she thought.

"Not much longer, my dear," said her mother as she fastened Felicity's coral necklace around her neck. "I'm almost through with you."

"Oh, Lissie," said Nan. "You look pretty. You really do."

Mrs. Merriman stepped back and studied Felicity from head to toe. Then she said, "Nan is right. Felicity Merriman, you look as pretty as can be." She looked pleased.

Felicity smiled. One of her garters was tied too tight. The laces on her bodice were tight, too. She felt nervous and uncomfortable and too clean, but it was almost worth it to see her mother so pleased.

"Off you go," said Mrs. Merriman. "It won't do
to be late to Miss Manderly's. And I won't have you
galloping there to arrive flushed and mussy." She gave
Felicity's hat one last touch. "Now remember to stop by
the store so Ben can escort you. And remember to sit up
straight."

"Remember your handkerchief!" added Nan.

"Go along, now," said Mrs. Merriman, shooing
Felicity toward the door. "Don't forget to speak softly.
Remember your gloves. And remember . . . " She
stopped.

Felicity looked back, waiting for her to finish.

"Remember that you are my dear daughter and I
am very proud of you," said Mrs. Merriman. "Now off
you go!"

Her mother's praise cheered Felicity as she hurried
along the busy street. Williamsburg was crowded now,
because it was Public Times. People from all over the
colony came to Williamsburg for business and pleasure
at Public Times. They came to hear the trials in the law
courts and to catch up on all the news. There were balls
and parties and markets and plays. The shops were

busy. The taverns were full of visitors from out of town. The streets were noisy with carts and carriages.

Felicity was glad to see that her father's store was bustling. She stood aside as two ladies stepped out the store's door.

"Terrible!" one lady said to the other. "Tea taxed at three pence a pound! Why, that raises the price high as a cat's back!"

"Indeed!" said the other lady. "The king's tax is unfair!"

Ben was the next person to come out of the store's door. He grinned at Felicity. "You look uncomfortable. Let's be on our way, so you can get your lessons over with," he said.

Felicity sighed. "I'd much rather stay at the store."

Ben stopped grinning. "The store is not so cheerful these days," he said.

"I just heard some ladies grumbling about the tax on tea," said Felicity.

"Aye," said Ben. "More and more people are complaining about the tax. They think the king is wrong to tax us colonists without our agreement."

"What do you think?" asked Felicity.

"I think the king's tax should be stopped," said Ben. "You'd better stop, too, or you'll get mud all over your petticoat." Ben pointed to a puddle in front of Felicity.

"Oh!" exclaimed Felicity impatiently, forgetting all about tea and taxes. She stepped around the puddle awkwardly. "I'm so dressed up I can hardly move. I wish being proper were not so uncomfortable! I wish I could have a lesson in whistling right now instead of a lesson in behaving like a lady."

"You'll whistle fine when that loose tooth falls out," said Ben. "How's it coming along? Shall I pull it for you?"

"No, thank you," said Felicity. "I'll wait for it to come out by itself."

"Just as well," said Ben. "Because here we are at Miss Manderly's door."

"Good-bye," said Felicity nervously. She touched her coral necklace for good luck, then knocked.

A smiling lady wearing a lacy white cap opened the door and greeted Felicity. "Miss Merriman?" she said. "How lovely to meet you. I am Miss Manderly."

There was something about Miss Manderly's eyes and the kindly way she tilted her head that made

Felicity feel a little less nervous. "Good day, madam," she said. "Thank you very much indeed for having me." *There,* she thought with relief, *I've done that much properly.*

"You are most welcome," said Miss Manderly. "Do come in and meet the other young ladies." She led Felicity into a sunny little parlor. Two girls rose from their chairs to greet her. One was very tall and dark-haired. The other was very small and fair-haired. Miss Manderly nodded to the tall girl. "Miss Felicity Merriman, may I present Miss Annabelle Cole," she said. Then she nodded to the smaller girl. "And this is Miss Elizabeth Cole."

"Oh, don't bother to call her Elizabeth," said the tall girl in a bossy way. "She's such a little bit of a thing, we call her 'Bitsy' at home."

Felicity thought Bitsy was a perfectly dreadful name. She could tell that Elizabeth hated it, too, though she said nothing. Felicity greeted the two girls. "Good day, Annabelle. Good day, *Elizabeth*," she said. She looked at Elizabeth and grinned. Elizabeth looked surprised.

Annabelle raised one eyebrow. "Your last name is

Merriman," she said. "You must be the shopkeeper's daughter." She sniffed, as if there were something wrong with being a shopkeeper's daughter.

Felicity was about to explain that her father's store was not a little shop, but one of the largest and finest stores in all of Williamsburg. But Annabelle turned her back. She flounced over to the writing desk and picked up her quill pen. "Of course, at home in England we had our own governess. I expect we shall have one here, too, if Mama can find a suitable person among the colonists," she said. Then she sighed, "I never thought we'd be taking lessons with a shopkeeper's daughter."

Felicity started to say that she was proud of being a colonist and very proud of her father's store, but Miss Manderly spoke first.

"Young ladies," said Miss Manderly. "Please be seated at the tea table." She sat herself gracefully and continued. "Your parents have trusted me with the important task of preparing you to take your place in society. Our lessons together will be pleasant. But do not forget that they are lessons. You are here to learn."

Felicity glanced over at Elizabeth. Her big blue eyes were open wide as she listened to Miss Manderly.

Miss Manderly went on. "Because it is our first
day together, we shall begin with polite conversation.
A lady makes her guests feel comfortable. She chats
pleasantly about topics that include everyone. It is
usually best to begin by asking a question of general
interest."

Annabelle spoke up. "*I* have a question of general
interest," she said. "Will the three of us always have our
lessons *together*?"

"Not all the time," answered Miss Manderly.

"Good," said Annabelle. "Because Bitsy and this
Miss Merriman are far behind me. My governess taught
me fine handwriting. I finished my sampler of stitches
long ago. And I had dancing lessons with the finest
dance master in England."

Miss Manderly smiled. "All of those skills improve
with practice," she said firmly. "And you are also
here to practice your best manners. I'm sure that your
governess in England taught you the rules of polite
behavior. So you know that if you are rude, and break
those rules, you will be left out of the best society."

All three girls sat up a little straighter. Miss Manderly paused as a maidservant placed a tea tray on the

table without rattling a cup. "Your manners will be observed most closely at tea," said Miss Manderly. "Tea is a ceremony. A gentlewoman must behave perfectly at the tea table, both as a hostess and as a guest. Now I will show you the proper way to serve tea."

"Good heavens!" said Annabelle. "Bitsy and I know how to serve tea! We've watched our mother serve tea hundreds of times!"

"Splendid!" said Miss Manderly calmly. "Then you will be quite at ease, won't you?"

Annabelle was quiet.

Miss Manderly opened the tea caddy made of dark, polished wood. Felicity smelled the spicy, smoky scent of tea. Miss Manderly neatly filled the silver caddy spoon five times and put the loose tea leaves into the delicate china teapot. Carefully, she poured hot water from the kettle onto the tea leaves. She put the pretty blue and gold lid on the teapot with a sure and grace-ful hand. Miss Manderly made it look so lovely that Felicity itched to try preparing the tea herself.

"Hand each guest her cup, saucer, and spoon," Miss Manderly said, as she did so. "And when the tea is ready, pour it very carefully." Felicity held her teacup

and saucer steady as Miss Manderly filled it. "Offer
your guest milk or sugar to put in her tea," said
Miss Manderly. "Then offer her a cake or a biscuit."

"Oh, these are queen cakes!" said Annabelle as she
took a small cake filled with currants from the plate. "I
have heard they are a favorite of the queen in England."

Miss Manderly held the plate of biscuits and queen
cakes out to Felicity. Felicity took the smallest biscuit
she saw. Miss Manderly smiled. "A wise choice. Hard
biscuits don't shed crumbs the way cakes do," she said.
"And remember, you are not drinking tea because you
are thirsty or eating because you are hungry. The tea is
offered to you as a sign of your hostess's hospitality. If
you refuse tea, you are refusing her generosity."

"Oh, I would never refuse!" Felicity said. "You
make the tea ceremony look so very *pretty*."

"Thank you, my dear," smiled Miss Manderly.
"But you may not wish to drink tea all afternoon! There
is a polite way to show that you have had *enough* tea.
Merely turn your cup upside down on your saucer and
place your spoon across it. That is a signal to your hostess that you do not wish to take more tea. And the correct phrase to say is, 'Thank you. I shall take no tea.'"

Felicity took a small bite of the hard biscuit. As soon as she chewed, she knew it was a mistake. Her loose tooth fell out and landed—plop! clink!—in her cup of tea. Felicity stared down at it. She didn't know what to do or say. No one else did either, not even Miss Manderly. The silence was very long.

Oh, dear, thought Felicity. *I'm sure dropping your tooth in your tea breaks all the rules of polite behavior!*

Felicity felt terrible. But then Elizabeth started to giggle quietly, in a way that made Felicity smile, then giggle with her.

Miss Manderly was laughing, too. Her eyes were sparkly. "Well!" she said. "I am afraid I do *not* know the polite thing to say when your tooth falls into your tea!" She turned to the maidservant. "Please take away Miss Merriman's teacup," she said. "But do return the tooth." Miss Manderly smiled, and Felicity felt fine.

When the tea tray was cleared away, Annabelle went off to practice writing fancy capital letters. Miss Manderly wrote out a phrase for Elizabeth and Felicity to copy into their copybooks:

*Think ere you speak,
for Words, once flown,
Once utter'd, are
no more your own.*

Miss Manderly sat back and read it aloud, "'Think ere you speak, for words, once flown, once uttered, are no more your own.' I would like you to practice writing this phrase," she said. "The word 'ere' means 'before.' The phrase tells you to think before you speak. And I think it is a good idea to think before you write, too." She smiled, then left to help Annabelle.

Felicity grinned at Elizabeth. "My mother is forever telling me to think before I speak and think before I act. She says I just gallop into everything with no more thought than a wild pony." Felicity dipped her quill pen in the inkwell she shared with Elizabeth. But instead of writing, she sketched a horse in her copybook.

Elizabeth looked at Felicity's sketch. "Oh, I love horses," she said. She asked shyly, "Do you?"

"More than anything," said Felicity. "Once I had a horse. I mean, once I had a horse for a while." She told Elizabeth about Penny. "I wanted to keep her, but she didn't belong to me. Her owner beat her, and she ran away. The truth is, I helped her run away. But I still think about her all the time."

Elizabeth's eyes were round and shiny. "That's the saddest, bravest thing I ever heard," she said. "Will Penny ever come back?"

"Maybe," said Felicity. "I hope so."

"I think she will," said Elizabeth firmly. "I'm sure she will, someday."

Felicity smiled at her. Elizabeth was going to be a good friend, a very good friend.

The girls were having such a good time writing and talking about horses, they were surprised when Miss Manderly said it was time to go home.

"Young ladies," said Miss Manderly. "At home this evening I would like you to practice writing invitations. Please pretend that you are inviting each other to tea. Write proper invitations in your copybooks. Use your best penmanship. At our next lesson, I will check your work. You may go now."

"Come along, Bitsy," said Annabelle in her bossy way.

Elizabeth started to say something to Annabelle, then waved and called, "Good day, Felicity!" instead.

"Good day, Elizabeth!" Felicity answered. She hurried home full of excitement. She could not wait to tell Mother and Nan about her afternoon.

Nan hopped up to greet Felicity when she came home. "What are the lessons like? And what is Miss Manderly like?" she asked eagerly.

"Miss Manderly is lovely," said Felicity. She sank into her chair with a happy sigh. "I hope I can learn to be like her."

"And the two girls from England?" asked Nan.

"The younger one, Elizabeth, is very fine," said Felicity. "She is just my age. But I don't like her older sister, Annabelle. She is a snob. She acts as if I am not as good as she is because my father owns a store. I'm supposed to write Annabelle an invitation to tea, to practice my writing. I'm not going to do it."

"You *must* do it," said Mrs. Merriman.

"Oh, but a proper invitation would say that I request the favor of her company," said Felicity. "And I don't *like* Annabelle's company."

Mrs. Merriman handed Felicity her copybook and the inkstand with the quill pen, inkwell, and sander. "We must often be with people we might not choose as company," said Mrs. Merriman. "A gentlewoman is kind to everyone."

"But Annabelle is rude," said Felicity. "She treated me badly because I am a colonist. She thinks colonists are uncivilized!"

"Then you must be perfectly polite," said Mrs. Merriman. "You must show her that we colonists are indeed civilized."

"Very well," grinned Felicity. She picked up the quill pen and dipped it in the ink. "I'll do it to show Annabelle how wrong she is."

Tea in the River

hy, Felicity!" exclaimed Miss Manderly at their next lesson. "Your invitations look lovely! What fine handwriting!" She handed back Felicity's copybook with a smile. Elizabeth smiled at Felicity, too.

Felicity beamed. She was proud of the invitations. She had practiced over and over again, until she was sure she could write the words perfectly. She forced herself to be slow and careful when she wrote in her copybook. Felicity was determined to show snobby Annabelle that she was just as accomplished and well mannered as any gentlewoman in England.

As the weeks went by, Felicity grew to enjoy her lessons with Miss Manderly more and more. She especially loved teatime. It was a peaceful part of the day when nothing rude or unsettling could happen. The

tea tray was beautiful, with blue china cups as delicate
as flowers and shiny spoons in the lovely china spoon
boat. Felicity memorized Miss Manderly's graceful
movements as she measured the tea out of the caddy.
She longed to use the caddy spoon and to pour the
steaming water into the pretty teapot. Sometimes
Miss Manderly asked her to hand around the cups and
offer the milk and sugar. Felicity was very careful. She
couldn't wait until it was her turn to prepare and pour
the tea herself. She wanted to do it perfectly.

Felicity still loved to run and play out of doors.
She was still quite often too lively to be ladylike. But
at lessons, Felicity tried to keep her voice low and her
back straight and her teacup balanced. She remembered
to laugh softly and ask polite questions. She began to
enjoy being on her best behavior at tea. Elizabeth and
Felicity always had a great deal to say to each other.
But Miss Manderly insisted they discuss questions of
general interest. That meant they had to include Annabelle in their conversations. Annabelle was not very interesting. But she usually tried to be pleasant at teatime.
She was almost always polite in front of Miss Manderly.

But one day at teatime, Miss Manderly left the room

for a moment. Annabelle heaved a big sigh. "Well," she said. "Soon we won't have any tea to drink if these uncivilized colonists have their way."

"What do you mean?" Felicity asked.

"Haven't you heard?" asked Annabelle in a mean voice. "A few days ago in Yorktown, a mob of colonists threw chests of tea into the river. The tea was on a ship that had come from England."

"But why did they do it?" asked Felicity.

"Because they are hot-heads!" said Annabelle. "They were a wild mob!"

"They didn't hurt anybody," Elizabeth said to Felicity softly.

"Quiet, Bitsy!" snapped Annabelle. Elizabeth shrank back. Annabelle went on. "The colonists destroyed the tea because they did not want to pay the king's tax on it. I've always said these colonists are ungrateful for all our king has done for them. I've always said—"

Just then, Miss Manderly returned. Annabelle stopped talking. She smiled sweetly at Miss Manderly.

Felicity did not know what to think. Could Annabelle be right? It was surely wrong for colonists to destroy tea they did not own. But wasn't the king's tax wrong, too? She looked down into her tea and said nothing.

Felicity was still quiet as she and Elizabeth walked home after lessons. They always hurried ahead of Annabelle so that they could talk.

"Lissie," said Elizabeth kindly. "It wasn't you or your family who threw the tea into the river. You shouldn't feel bad about what those other colonists did. It's not your fault."

"I know," said Felicity. "But Annabelle makes me so angry. She thinks colonists are no good."

Elizabeth smiled a little. "I know one colonist Annabelle admires," she said quietly. "Your father's apprentice."

Felicity stopped. "Ben?" she asked. "Annabelle likes Ben?"

"Aye," nodded Elizabeth. "Annabelle thinks he is handsome. And she found out that he is from a wealthy family. So she admires him."

Felicity laughed. "So that's why she lurks around the store and flutters her eyelashes at Ben like a ninny. Wait till Ben finds out that Annabelle is sweet on him!"

"Oh, you mustn't tell him!" said Elizabeth. "Annabelle would be so angry if you did!"

"I won't tell Ben," said Felicity. "Don't worry."

Felicity and Elizabeth waited at Mr. Merriman's store for Annabelle to catch up. They chatted about their lessons, and horses, and their samplers. But whenever they thought about Annabelle being sweet on Ben, they began to giggle. It was very hard not to laugh when Annabelle came into the store. She looked around. When she saw Ben was not there, she said briskly, "Come along, Bitsy! There's no need to stay!"

Felicity and Elizabeth smiled at each other and waved good-bye.

Soon after Elizabeth and Annabelle had left, Mr. Merriman began to close up the store. "You and Elizabeth are the merriest girls in Virginia," he said. "You always have a great deal to talk about."

"Aye," said Felicity. "Today we had a wonderful idea for something to put on our samplers. Miss Manderly says we're to start them soon. We are going to need lots of red silk thread."

"Are you going to stitch some red Virginia roses, red as the roses in my lovely Lissie's cheeks?" asked Mr. Merriman.

"Oh, no," said Felicity. "Elizabeth says we should put a bright red crown right at the top of our samplers to show that we all look up to the same king. She says that he is fair and generous to everyone he rules, in England and in his colonies."

"Well," said Mr. Merriman with a sad smile. "I am not sure everyone would agree. Many people feel the king is treating us colonists badly. They do not want to be ruled by the king anymore."

Felicity was confused. "But isn't that *disloyal*?" she asked.

Mr. Merriman shrugged. "People will not be loyal to someone who treats them unfairly. And they feel the king's tax on tea is unfair."

"Annabelle said some colonists threw tea into the York River," said Felicity. "Is that true?"

"Yes," said Mr. Merriman. "It was their way of showing the king they are angry. Other people have decided they are not going to buy tea or even drink it anymore. That will be *their* way to show the king that they are angry."

"Just because they have to pay a few pence more for tea?" asked Felicity.

"It isn't only the tax on tea," answered Mr. Merriman. "We colonists built this country with our own hard work. Many people feel we should govern it ourselves, without the king."

Without the king? Felicity couldn't imagine it. "Do you think we would be better off without the king, Father?" she asked.

Mr. Merriman sighed. "That is the question everyone is asking."

Felicity looked up at him. "Miss Manderly would call it a question of general interest," she said.

"Quite so," said Mr. Merriman. "And I do not know the answer to it."

"Well, do you think I should not stitch a crown on my sampler?" Felicity asked her father.

Mr. Merriman handed her some red silk thread. "I think you must answer that question for yourself," he said. "Now come along, my child. 'Tis time we were on our way home."

Bananabelle

Felicity did not say anything to Elizabeth about the talk she'd had with her father about the king and tea. She was too confused and uncomfortable. She did not decide what to do about her sampler, either. She made a few stitches with the red thread at the top of her sampler, but they didn't look like a crown, that was for certain. They looked like bumpy knots.

"Oh, no!" she exclaimed. "I've tangled my thread *again*! I shall have to cut it and start all over." She and Elizabeth were working on their samplers at Elizabeth's house one cold November afternoon.

"My mother has some scissors in her chamber," said Elizabeth. "Let's go and fetch them."

"Will we disturb your mother?" asked Felicity.

"Oh, no," said Elizabeth. "She and Annabelle have

gone out calling. They won't be home for hours. Follow me."

Felicity and Elizabeth went up the wide staircase to Mrs. Cole's bedchamber. "She keeps the scissors in her sewing basket," said Elizabeth. "Over here, next to her wigs."

"I've never seen so many wigs and curls outside the wigmaker's shop," said Felicity. She looked at the five carved, wooden heads lined up in a row. "Do you think I might try a wig on?" she asked boldly.

"Well, I suppose so," said Elizabeth.

Felicity took a wig of dark hair off one of the heads. "I have always wanted to see what I would look like with dark hair," she said. She gazed at herself in the looking glass and giggled. "I look like a ninny!"

Elizabeth giggled. "Oh, Lissie, you *do* look funny!"

Felicity loved to make Elizabeth laugh. She picked up the bald wooden head and fluttered her eyelashes at it, just like Annabelle. "Oh, my darling Ben!" she said in a high voice. "It is I, your beautiful Bananabelle! You have stolen my heart away!"

"Bananabelle!" Elizabeth laughed. "You sound just like her!"

Felicity pressed her cheek against the wooden head's cheek. "Let us be married, my darling Ben. And we can discuss questions of general interest all the day long! Oh, I love you, you handsome lad! Say that you love me, your Bananabelle, or I shall die!" She gave the wooden head a big, smacking kiss.

"WHAT'S *THIS*?" Annabelle's voice boomed from the doorway.

Felicity pulled off the wig and whirled around. Elizabeth went white.

Annabelle crossed her arms. "So this is what you and your rude little shopkeeper friend do, Bitsy?"

Elizabeth did not say anything. She looked down at her shoes.

Felicity said, "Oh, Annabelle. It was only a bit of fun."

"Fun?" snorted Annabelle. "You have no manners! I shall tell Mama what you've done. We shall see if she thinks it is fun. I wouldn't be surprised if she tells Bitsy never to speak to you again!"

Felicity was not afraid of Annabelle. "If you tell your mother," she said coolly, "I will tell Ben you are sweet on him."

"Oh!" sputtered Annabelle. "Oh!" She glared at Felicity. "You . . . you uncivilized brat!" She stormed from the room.

Elizabeth looked at Felicity. Her blue eyes were troubled. "Why did you say that to her?" she asked. "Now she will be angry."

Felicity shrugged. "She is nothing but a bully. I don't care if she is angry. She doesn't scare me. She shouldn't scare you."

"But I'm not like you, Felicity," said Elizabeth. "I'm not brave. Annabelle can be mean sometimes. I've always been afraid of her."

"You don't have to be afraid of her anymore," said Felicity. "I am your friend now. I'll help you. I am not afraid of old Bananabelle."

At last, Elizabeth smiled. "Lissie," she said, "I'm so glad we're friends."

"Me, too," said Felicity. "But I'd best go along now. Will you walk with me?"

The girls pulled their cloaks close around them, for the wind was sharp. They hurried along to Mr. Merriman's store and ran inside, all out of breath. "Stay for a moment to get warm," Felicity said to Elizabeth.

There were six well-dressed men talking to Mr. Merriman and Ben. One of the men was holding a paper that had a long list of names on it. No one noticed the girls as they slipped into a corner by the fireplace and warmed their hands. Felicity looked up in surprise when she heard her father speaking. He sounded very stern, though his voice was steady.

"Yes, I signed the agreement," said Mr. Merriman. "More than four hundred other merchants around the colonies signed it, too. We have decided not to sell tea anymore. It is our way of showing the king we think the tax on tea is wrong."

"That is disloyal!" shouted one man. "It is wrong for colonists to go against the king! You know it is wrong, Merriman."

Elizabeth and Felicity hid behind a barrel. They were very quiet.

"Gentlemen," said Mr. Merriman firmly. "Do not tell me what to do in my store. I will do what my heart and my reason tell me is right."

"And what of those hot-heads in Yorktown? Do you think they were right to toss good tea into the river?" said another man.

"They threw that tea away to send a message to the king," said Mr. Merriman. "They did what they thought was right."

"They were *wrong* to toss that tea!" said the man angrily. "And you are wrong to stop selling tea."

"Aye!" said another man. "You are making a grave mistake. You'll get no more of my money, Merriman. None of us will ever shop here again! We won't give our business to anyone who isn't loyal to the king. Will we, gentlemen?"

"No!" called out several of the men. The store shook with their shouts.

Felicity turned to Elizabeth, but she was gone.

Mr. Merriman's voice was sad. "You gentlemen are my neighbors and my friends," he said as the men left. "I had hoped we could disagree politely, without fighting. Fighting does no good."

Felicity stayed in the corner until all the men were gone and the store was quiet. Her father and Ben were standing silently. Felicity ran up to her father and hugged him. "Father!" she said.

Mr. Merriman held her close. "Did you hear that, my child?" he asked.

"Aye," said Felicity. "Elizabeth and I both did."

"And did it frighten you?" asked Mr. Merriman.

"A little," said Felicity. "Who were those men, Father?"

"Just some men of the town," said her father. "I know most of them."

Ben spoke up. "They are Loyalists," he said. "They are angry because some of us have joined together to protest against the king."

"I've decided to stop selling tea in my store, to show the king we colonists will not pay his tax," explained Mr. Merriman.

"If no one pays the tax, it will make the king angry," said Felicity. "Won't that start a fight?"

"Aye," said Mr. Merriman softly. "It could."

"Do you think there will be a war?" asked Felicity.

"I don't know," said Mr. Merriman, shaking his head.

"It may take a war to show the king he cannot treat the colonists this way anymore!" exclaimed Ben.

"Hush, boy!" said Mr. Merriman. "You have not seen war, as I have. War is the worst way to solve disagreements. War is like a terrible illness. Everyone suffers. People die. Those who survive are weakened, and 'tis a long while before they are full strength again."

Ben was quiet. Felicity was quiet, too. Then she asked, "Father, will we drink tea at home?"

"No," said Mr. Merriman. "There will be no tea in our house."

"But what should I do at lessons?" asked Felicity. "We drink tea there. And teatime is so very *important*. What will Miss Manderly think if I refuse tea?" She turned to her father with a sad, confused face.

A Bright Red Cardinal Bird

&❧ CHAPTER 10 ❦❧

 elicity and Elizabeth did not have a chance to talk at lessons the next day. Miss Manderly was working with them on their samplers.

"And what is this at the top of your sampler, Felicity?" Miss Manderly asked. "Such bright red thread. Perhaps you are stitching our Virginia song-bird, the cardinal. Is that what you are planning?"

"I . . . I don't know," said Felicity. "I haven't decided."

"Well," said Miss Manderly. "You will have to decide soon, my dear. You cannot leave red knots at the top of your sampler!"

Felicity saw Elizabeth looking at her. The red crown on Elizabeth's sampler was almost finished.

When it was time for tea, Miss Manderly smiled.

"Young ladies," she said, "you have made such fine progress. I think the time has come for you to take turns serving the tea. Annabelle, you are the eldest. You shall serve the tea today."

Felicity was nervous. She had not decided what she was going to do about tea, either. Her family wasn't drinking tea at home. Should she drink it here? She watched as Annabelle sat behind the tea table acting very important. After Annabelle prepared the tea, she filled Miss Manderly's cup first, then Elizabeth's cup, and then her own.

Miss Manderly leaned forward in her chair. "Annabelle, my dear," she said. "You have forgotten to serve Miss Merriman her tea."

"Oh!" said Annabelle, holding her cup daintily. "I was only thinking of the carpet."

"The carpet?" asked Miss Manderly.

"Yes, indeed," said Annabelle. She put her nose in the air. "I did not serve Felicity because I did not want her to toss the tea out all over your fine carpet."

Felicity felt her face getting red.

"Annabelle!" gasped Miss Manderly. "Apologize at once!"

"Oh, but Felicity would be proud to toss out her tea," said Annabelle. "Her father said it was *right* to toss out tea. He said those hot-heads in Yorktown were right to throw the tea into the river."

"No!" cried Felicity. "My father didn't say that! He—"

"Yes, he did!" snapped Annabelle. "Bitsy heard him. Didn't you, Bitsy?"

Elizabeth didn't say anything.

"But that's *not* what he said," cried Felicity. "Tell her, Elizabeth!"

Elizabeth would not look at Felicity.

Felicity tried to explain. "My father said the men who threw the tea into the river thought that they were right. They did it to show the king that they did not agree with the tax on tea."

"Your father disagrees with the king's tax, too!" said Annabelle. "That's why he's not going to sell tea in his store anymore. He is disloyal to the king. Your father is a *traitor*!"

"No!" shouted Felicity. "My father is not a traitor!" She jumped up from her chair and knocked against the tea tray. The teapot teetered and the cups and saucers rattled. Felicity grabbed her sampler frame in her fist and ran out of the room. She slammed the door behind her.

Felicity was in a red rage. Home she stormed, away from Miss Manderly's prim little house, through the crowded, dusty streets. *How could Elizabeth do it? How could she?* she kept asking herself. It was Elizabeth she was most angry at. *Why didn't she tell Annabelle the truth? Father was only trying to be fair. Father is not the one who is a traitor,* thought Felicity. *Elizabeth is the traitor— to me!*

Felicity burst into the house and pounded up the stairs to her room. She curled up on her bed in a tight roll. Her sampler was loosened and wrinkled. She could not think. She was too mad to cry. Anger boiled inside her. Elizabeth was supposed to be her friend. Instead, she let Annabelle tell hateful lies about her father. *I hate Annabelle,* she thought, *and I hate Elizabeth, too. I don't want to see either of them ever again.*

Felicity heard the door open. "Lissie?" whispered her mother. She sat on the bed and put Felicity's head in her lap. "What is it, my child?" her mother asked softly. She smoothed Felicity's hair. "What is it, Lissie?"

Felicity took a shaky breath. "Elizabeth and Annabelle think Father is a traitor. I don't want to speak to them ever again," she said.

"Ahhhh," said her mother sadly. "It's because of the argument about tea, isn't it?"

Felicity sat up and nodded.

Mrs. Merriman sighed. "My poor child," she said. "I fear there is more of this trouble coming. This talk against the king will cause nothing but sorrow before it is over. It will divide families and destroy friendships, if we let it." Gently, she took Felicity's sampler from her hands.

"Throw that away!" said Felicity. "I hate it. It is full of mistakes."

Mrs. Merriman pulled the sampler taut in its frame. "No, my impatient one," she said calmly. "I see a great deal that's good in this sampler. It would be a terrible waste to throw it all away because of one mistake or two." She looked at Felicity. "I think it would be a terrible waste to throw away your friendship with Elizabeth, too, because of one misunderstanding."

"How can I be Elizabeth's friend?" asked Felicity. "She thinks Father is a traitor to the king!"

"Did she say that?" asked her mother.

"No, Annabelle did. But Elizabeth did not stop her," said Felicity.

"Elizabeth is not as brave as you are," said Mother. "You must be patient with your friend, Lissie."

"She's not my friend!" said Felicity. "If she were my friend, she wouldn't have let Annabelle say such awful things!"

"I see," said Mother. "You are afraid Elizabeth does not like you anymore. Is that it?"

"Aye," whispered Felicity.

"I think you are wrong about that," said Mrs. Merriman. "But you will have to go back to your lessons to find out."

"I don't want to go to the lessons anymore!" exclaimed Felicity.

"They are a privilege," said Mrs. Merriman. "It is not wise to walk away from such a chance to learn."

"I want to forget everything I've learned," said Felicity.

"Aye," said Mrs. Merriman, looking down at the sampler. "It is easiest to throw everything away. It is harder to untangle knots and try again." She looked at Felicity with love. "It takes courage."

Felicity thought for a moment. Then she said, "What if I *do* go back? What shall I do when they serve tea? I want to be loyal to Father. I don't want to drink tea anymore. But if I am rude, Miss Manderly won't want me to come back ever again. Elizabeth won't want to be my friend. And Annabelle will think she is right, that colonists *are* uncivilized." Felicity looked at her mother. "What shall I do?"

"Now that is a difficult knot to untangle," said Mrs. Merriman. "You must be well mannered but follow your heart. You must be polite but do what you think is right." She handed the sampler back to Felicity. "I trust you will find a way. You have become quite a gracious young lady these past few weeks." Mrs. Merriman kissed Felicity's forehead and left quietly.

It took all the bravery Felicity could muster to walk back into Miss Manderly's house the next day.

Miss Manderly greeted her with a smile. "Good day, Miss Merriman," she said. "I am exceedingly glad to see you today."

"Thank you, Miss Manderly," Felicity said. She sat down and went to work on her sampler. She did not speak to Elizabeth or Annabelle. They did not speak to her.

"Why, Felicity, how lovely," said Miss Manderly. "I see that you have indeed stitched a red cardinal bird at the top of your sampler. It looks just like our proud Virginia cardinals!"

"Oh!" said Elizabeth. "It *is* pretty, Lissie." She looked at Felicity shyly. "Would you mind, I mean, do you think it would be all right if I stitched one just like it on my sampler?" she asked.

"Bitsy!" scolded Annabelle.

Elizabeth whirled around and faced Annabelle. "I *hate* being called Bitsy," she said firmly. "From now on, call me *Elizabeth*."

"Why, I—" sputtered Annabelle.

"Or I will call you Bananabelle in front of everyone," said Elizabeth. "Annabelle, Bananabelle."

For once, Annabelle was speechless. Elizabeth grinned at Felicity. Felicity felt her spirits rise like a bird. *Elizabeth is still my friend,* she thought. She smiled at Elizabeth.

Miss Manderly smiled, too. "Well, *Elizabeth*," she said. "Will you do us the honor of serving tea this afternoon?"

"Yes, indeed!" said Elizabeth.

Felicity's heart pounded as she took her place at the tea table. This was the moment she dreaded. How could she refuse tea without being rude? She watched Elizabeth measure the tea and pour the hot water into the teapot. She watched as Elizabeth handed each of them a teacup, saucer, and spoon. Then Elizabeth began to fill the teacups. She poured Miss Manderly's cup without spilling a drop. She poured Annabelle's cup and offered her the sugar. Felicity's cup was next.

Felicity took a deep breath. Very gracefully, she turned her teacup upside down on the saucer and put her spoon across it. "Thank you, Elizabeth," she said politely in a clear, strong voice. "I shall take no tea."

"Well done," said Miss Manderly softly.

Elizabeth smiled. "Perhaps you'd like a queen cake," she said as she handed the plate to Felicity.

"I'd prefer a plain biscuit," said Felicity as she smiled back at her friend. "I've no loose teeth to worry about today!"

An Invitation to the Palace

elicity ran along the frozen path as if she were running toward Christmas. Then quick! She turned sideways and slid, slick as a fish, across a smooth stretch of ice. "Try sliding!" she called back to Nan. "It's *fast*! I'm going to do it again!"

Nan grinned but shook her head. "We shouldn't slide, Lissie. It isn't proper," she said. "And anyway, you know we promised Mother we wouldn't play. We said we'd come straight home after we cut enough holly to fill our baskets."

"Very well," said Felicity cheerfully. She knew Nan was right, as usual. Besides, she had already spotted more clear patches of ice ahead. So she ran and slid, ran and slid, while Nan trotted along behind, carefully picking up the holly sprigs that fell out of Felicity's basket.

"Mother! William!" called Felicity as she and Nan burst into the house. "Come see the holly we've cut. 'Tis ever so full of berries!"

Mrs. Merriman and little William hurried to greet the girls.

"Look at all the holly!" said William. "A lot and a lot!"

Mrs. Merriman smiled. "My two Christmas sprites!" she said. "You *have* done a fine job. The holly is perfect. Now I can work Christmas magic on the house. But look at you! Your noses are as red and cold as the holly berries.

"Go sit yourselves by the fire. Lissie, take your shoes off first. Don't track that muddy slush into the parlor." She scooped up William with one arm and the two holly baskets with the other. "Later, you can help me decorate. It will be a fine surprise for your father and Ben."

Just then, they heard polite knocking on the door. "Oh, Lissie," said Mrs. Merriman. "My hands are full. Do please answer the door."

"Yes, Mother," said Felicity. The floor was slippery, and she slid a little as she hurried to the door. When she opened it, she stepped back in surprise. "Goodness!" she gasped.

There stood a very elegantly dressed man. He bowed to Mrs. Merriman. "Good day, madam," he said. "Do I have the honor of addressing the wife of Mr. Edward Merriman?" Felicity's mother nodded, and the man held out a letter. "This is for you, madam," he said.

Mrs. Merriman quickly put William and the holly baskets down and took the letter. "Thank you," she said as the man left. "Good day to you."

Felicity, Nan, and William crowded close to Mother as she untied the red ribbon and opened the letter. "Why, Lissie!" she exclaimed. "It is from Lady Dunmore, the royal governor's wife. It's an invitation for *you*."

"Me?" gasped Felicity.

"Just listen," said Mrs. Merriman. She cleared her throat and read the invitation. "Lady Dunmore presents her compliments to Mrs. Merriman and requests the favor of her daughter Felicity's attendance at a dancing lesson at the Palace on Saturday, January seven at four o'clock."

"Oooh, Lissie!" sighed Nan. "You are so lucky!"

Mother handed the invitation to Felicity. She read it, but she could hardly believe the message written in curlicues and fancy script. *She* was invited to the royal Governor's Palace. The Palace was the fanciest, most *elegant* place in Williamsburg. Many times she'd peeked through the iron gates in the high brick wall around it. And now she was invited to come inside, as a guest! Felicity was speechless. The room was so quiet, they all jumped when they heard more knocking at the door.

"Whatever now?" laughed Mrs. Merriman. "I shouldn't be surprised if it's King George himself!"

But it was Elizabeth, waving an invitation just like Felicity's. "Oh, you got yours, too!" she exclaimed. Her blue eyes were bright with excitement. "Isn't it wonderful? Both of us invited to the Palace! Won't it be grand? A dance lesson isn't like a school lesson. There will be music, and lovely food, and everyone wearing beautiful clothes. This dance lesson will be almost like a ball!"

"A ball!" said Nan, wide-eyed.

Elizabeth rattled on, "My mother says Miss Manderly arranged for us to be invited. Miss Manderly knows the dancing master who teaches the governor's children. She asked him to invite you and me and Annabelle. Aren't you excited?"

"Yes!" laughed Felicity. "I think I must be in a dream."

"The cold will wake you from your dream," smiled Mrs. Merriman. "Put your shoes back on, Lissie. Go to the store and show the invitation to your father. You must ask his permission to go to the dancing lesson. Hurry now."

Felicity pulled her shoes back on. "Can you come to the store with me, Elizabeth?" she asked.

"No, I'd best not," Elizabeth answered. "My mother doesn't like me to be out in the cold. She's certain I'll catch a fever." The two girls shared a look that said, *Aren't mothers silly, always worried about fevers and such?* Then Elizabeth left for home.

Felicity gave no thought to the cold as she stepped out into the twilight. There was a happy feeling in the city of Williamsburg that evening. Windows in many of the houses and shops were trimmed inside with holiday greenery as if they were dressed up for a special occasion. Some wore necklaces of ivy. Others had fans of pine or garlands of holly leaves.

Christmastide was Felicity's favorite time of year. It was the season of celebrations, pretty decorations, and many visitors. And this Christmas promised to be the most wonderful ever. This Christmas Felicity was invited to the Palace! Felicity held her invitation safe under her cloak and hurried toward her father's store.

The store was empty of customers, though it was not yet closing time. Since Mr. Merriman had stopped selling tea, the store was never very busy. People who agreed with the king had stopped shopping there. Felicity stepped into the shadowy store lit by a few flickering candles. She called out, "Hello! Hello!"

"Hello, yourself!" answered a cheery voice. It was Ben. He was up on a ladder, dusting high shelves. He grinned down at Felicity. "This is a fine surprise," he said. "Have you come for a whistling lesson?"

"Not this time," laughed Felicity. "Where's Father?"

"In his counting room," said Ben. "What's happened?"

"Oh, nothing!" said Felicity airily. "Only the very finest thing ever in the world!"

"And what might that be?" laughed Ben.

But Felicity did not answer him, because she saw

her father coming. "Father! Look!" she cried as she ran toward him, waving the invitation. "Elizabeth and Annabelle and I have been invited to the Palace!"

"To the Palace?" Mr. Merriman exclaimed. He opened the invitation and held it near the candlelight. Ben climbed down the ladder and came to take a look, too.

"May I go, Father? Elizabeth says it will be almost like a ball!" said Felicity, placing her hand on his arm. "Oh, please say I can go!"

"Well, I . . ." her father began.

"Lissie!" Ben burst out before Mr. Merriman could finish. "How can you even *consider* it? How could you possibly go to the Governor's Palace? How could you smile at the governor and drink his punch as if you're the best of friends? How *could* you?"

"I'm not angry at the governor," Felicity said hotly.

"You should be!" said Ben. "You know Governor Dunmore represents the king here in Virginia. You know the king and the governor have treated us colonists badly!"

"Well," said Felicity. "I suppose so, but . . ."

Ben didn't listen. "If you go to this dance lesson,

you'll be surrounded by Loyalists," he said. "You'll be dancing with children of the very same people who have snubbed us and refused to shop at your father's store ever since we stopped selling tea." Ben shook his head. "Don't you see, Lissie? You can't go. You *can't*."

Felicity felt plunged in gloom. She understood everything Ben was saying, but she still wanted to go to the dance lesson. She looked at her father. "*Is* it wrong for me to go to the Palace, Father?" she asked.

Mr. Merriman looked down into Felicity's sad face. "Lissie, my dear," he said. "I think it is wrong when adults' arguments make children unhappy. The invitation is kind. The governor and his lady are parents, just as I am. They want their children to be happy, especially at Christmastide. Christmas is not the time for anger. It is the time for friendliness and good spirit and merriment, too."

"So you say she should go, sir?" asked Ben. He sounded surprised.

"Indeed, yes. I *do* think Felicity should go to the Governor's Palace," answered Mr. Merriman. "And she should dance with the governor's children and their friends. Because if our children can dance together, then perhaps we adults can settle our differences without fighting."

Felicity smiled at her father. "Oh, thank you, Father," she said. "I did so hope you would say I could go."

Mr. Merriman smiled, too. "Christmas is the time our hopes for peace and happiness should come true," he said.

Felicity looked at Ben. She hoped Father had made him think that it was right for her to go to the dance lesson. But Ben was frowning. Felicity knew she had disappointed him. "Ben," she began, "It's *Christmas* . . ."

Ben turned sharply and walked away, out of the candlelight.

Sugar Cakes and Christmas Hopes

heerful sunlight shone through the windows into the kitchen. Felicity and Elizabeth were having a merry, messy time baking Shrewsbury cakes. Elizabeth was beating an egg and rose water together in a bowl. Felicity had unwrapped the blue paper from a sugar loaf and scraped off a cup of sugar.

"Five days till Christmas," said Felicity. "And then thirteen days till we go to the Palace. It seems such a terribly long time to wait."

"Yes!" agreed Elizabeth. She added a pinch of nutmeg to the bowl. "I think about the dance lesson *all* the time."

Felicity spooned the sugar into Elizabeth's bowl. "When you lived in England, did you ever go to a dance lesson as fancy as this one will be?" she asked.

"Oh, no!" said Elizabeth. "Never anything as grand

as this! Mother says it is such a special occasion, Annabelle and I will ride to the Palace in a carriage. We shall
each have a footman to escort us right up to the Palace
door. Who will escort you, Lissie?"

"I don't know," said Felicity. "Most likely my father
will."

Elizabeth grinned. "I have a fine idea!" she said.
"*Ben* could escort you to the Palace. That would make
Annabelle green with envy!"

Elizabeth and Felicity usually giggled at the idea
of Annabelle trying to make Ben notice her. So Elizabeth looked surprised when Felicity frowned and said
sharply, "No! Ben will *not* escort me to the Palace."

"But why not?" asked Elizabeth. "He is your
friend."

Felicity thumped the dough hard with the rolling
pin. "Ben does not think I should go to the dance lesson
at the Palace at all," she said. "He is angry at the governor and the Loyalists. He thinks I should be angry, too."

"Oh," said Elizabeth softly. Elizabeth's parents were
Loyalists. Her father was friendly with the governor.

"But my father said the governor and his lady were
kind to invite me, and that I should go," said Felicity.

"He said Christmas is the time when our hopes for peace and happiness should come true."

"Well, that's a good thing," said Elizabeth. She sounded relieved. "Because it would be terrible if you couldn't go. I wouldn't even *like* the dance lesson if you were not there."

"Don't worry!" said Felicity with a grin. "I'll be there! I promise!" She wiped her floury hands on her apron. "Now, then," she asked, "which cake cutter do you want to use first? The star, the moon, the heart, or the clover?"

"Oh, the star," said Elizabeth. "I want to use the Christmas star first."

That afternoon, Felicity brought a pretty basket of the Shrewsbury cakes she and Elizabeth had made to lessons at Miss Manderly's house.

"Such lovely cakes," said Miss Manderly. "Thank you, Felicity."

"Elizabeth and I made them," said Felicity. "We wanted to thank you for our invitations to the dance lesson. I never dreamed I would be invited to the Palace. 'Tis a great honor."

"I'm glad you are pleased," said Miss Manderly.

"I know you young ladies will do honor to your parents and to my instruction."

"Do you suppose we will be presented to Governor and Lady Dunmore?" asked Elizabeth. "Will we be introduced to them?"

"Perhaps," said Miss Manderly.

"Well," said Annabelle in a snooty voice. "If we *are* introduced, Governor and Lady Dunmore will know who Elizabeth and I are. They know our father. When they hear our last name, they will know we are from a family of Loyalists."

Governor and Lady Dunmore may know of my father, too, thought Felicity. *When they hear my last name, they will know I am not from a family of Loyalists. Maybe they won't like me.* She felt a little nervous.

"The governor and his lady will care more about your manners than your name," said Miss Manderly. "We must practice making a curtsy so that you will make a good impression if you are introduced."

Miss Manderly had taught the girls to make a curtsy in order to show their respect when they met someone important. Now Felicity stood with Annabelle and Elizabeth to practice. Miss Manderly reminded them of the movements.

"Stand with your back straight and put one foot slightly in front of the other," said Miss Manderly as she watched them. "Your head should be bowed and tilted to the side a bit. Eyes looking down, Annabelle. 'Tis rude to stare boldly. Now sink down. Slowly! And say softly, 'My lord. My lady.' And then rise. Quite good! But Felicity, don't sink so low. Then you will not wobble. You don't want to fall in a heap at the governor's feet!"

"No, Miss Manderly," said Felicity.

"Oh!" tittered Annabelle. "Can you imagine what an embarrassment it would be to fall!" She looked at Felicity out of the corner of her eye. "I have heard that the dance master is very strict," she prattled on. "He struck two girls because they made mistakes in the dance! And once he scolded a young man sharply because his manner was not quite correct."

"That's enough, Annabelle," said Miss Manderly. "You will all dance beautifully, especially if you practice between now and the day of the dance lesson." She sat at the spinet. "Let us begin our dance practice now. Then none of you need worry."

But Felicity *was* worried. She knew she was not good at dancing. And today she was worse than usual. She even stepped on Elizabeth's toe! What if she should step on the toe of one of the governor's sons! Soon Felicity was so busy worrying, she lost track of the dance entirely. Elizabeth tried to help by whispering instructions to her.

"Point your toe!" Elizabeth whispered. She counted the steps for Felicity in a soft voice. "Step on one, sink down on two, step three, four, five. Sink down on six. Now backwards!"

But Felicity was red-faced and fussed. She just couldn't get back in step. It seemed like hours before Miss Manderly said dance practice was over and they could all go.

As they were walking home, Felicity said to Elizabeth, "I was so excited about going to the Palace, I forgot the invitation was for a dance lesson. If we were going to run races or ride horses, then I know I would do well. But I am terrible at dancing."

"Silly old Annabelle made you nervous today with all her talk about the strict dance master," Elizabeth said calmly. "You'll do fine at the Palace."

"No I won't!" exclaimed Felicity. She turned to her friend. "Oh, Elizabeth," she said desperately, "I want to go to the dance lesson at the Palace more than anything in the world. But . . . but the truth is, I am afraid."

"Afraid!" said Elizabeth. "Why, Felicity, you're the bravest girl I know!"

Felicity shook her head. "Not this time," she said. "I'm afraid I will look like a fool."

"You will *not* look like a fool," said Elizabeth loyally. "You will look beautiful. I can imagine it. You will make a curtsy perfectly. The governor and his lady will be charmed. And you will dance like a dream. Your gown will be all shiny in the candlelight. Your petticoats will swirl around you. And everyone will say, who is that graceful and elegant young lady?"

Felicity grinned. When Elizabeth described the scene, she could almost see herself looking elegant at the Palace.

"What are you going to wear?" asked Elizabeth.

The question brought Felicity back to earth. "Oh," she said. "I hadn't thought about that. I'll wear my brown silk gown, I suppose."

"The one you wear to church every Sunday?" Elizabeth asked.

"Yes," said Felicity. "It's my best."

"Oh, yes, of course," said Elizabeth quickly. "That gown always looks fine. You will be comfortable, too, because it's not—it's not so awfully fancy. And you are used to wearing it because it is not new."

"Are you going to wear a new gown?" Felicity asked.

"No, no," said Elizabeth. "It's not new. Well, it is new to *me*. It is one of Annabelle's old silk gowns. My mother is making a new stomacher for it and trimming it with new lace."

"It sounds most elegant," said Felicity wistfully.

Elizabeth shrugged as if she wanted Felicity to think she did not care about clothes. "My mother and Annabelle say that Lady Dunmore is the most fashionable lady in all the colonies," she said. "They are making a fuss about the gowns. I don't think clothes are so terribly important."

That is what Elizabeth said, but Felicity could tell she did not really mean it. Felicity knew Elizabeth thought it was very important to wear a wonderful gown to the Palace. Felicity did not usually pay much attention to clothes. But now she began to think Elizabeth was absolutely right.

"If I had a beautiful new gown I wouldn't be nervous," said Felicity. "Then I would dance well. I would not make any mistakes. If I had a new gown, everything would be perfect."

Elizabeth asked, "Do you think you might have one if you asked your mother?"

"I don't think so," Felicity said sadly. "My mother is so busy just now, getting ready for Christmas. And she and my father are worried about money. There hasn't been much business at the store of late."

"Oh," said Elizabeth. She was quiet. Then she said, "Well . . . well, you might just *ask*. Remember what your father said about hopes coming true at Christmastide."

"Perhaps," said Felicity, "perhaps." Felicity thought *asking* for a new gown just now would be selfish. But she could not help *hoping* for one.

Tidings of Comfort and Joy

*T*he next morning, Mrs. Merriman said, "Felicity, come along with me. I'm going to the apothecary to get medicine for my cough. We can stop by the milliner on the way home. Perhaps we can find some trim or lace to spruce up your brown silk gown for the dance lesson at the Palace. Would you fancy that?"

"Yes, Mother," said Felicity. She tried to sound pleased. But she was thinking, *Even with new trim, I will still look like a little brown field mouse!*

Felicity trailed along with her mother from shop to shop. She was thinking so hard about asking for a new gown, she only half heard the apothecary and her mother chatting.

"Mrs. Merriman," said Mr. Galt, the apothecary, "I am concerned about your cough. It should not linger

for weeks as it has. I shall give you garlic syrup and
some licorice lozenges. But you must rest."

"Thank you, Mr. Galt," said Mrs. Merriman. "I'll
have plenty of time to rest after Christmas. 'Tis such a
happy, busy time just now!"

Mr. Galt shook his head. "I fear your cough will
turn into something more serious if you do not take
care," he said. "Mind you, wrap up well. 'Tis frightfully
cold."

"Aye!" said Mrs. Merriman. "The cold cuts straight
to my bones!" She coughed as she turned to go. "Come
along, Lissie," she said. "Good day, Mr. Galt. I wish you
joy of the season!"

Felicity and her mother hurried to the milliner's
shop. Usually, Felicity was not very interested in the
pretty shop full of finery for ladies and gentlemen.
Never before had Felicity paid attention to the feathers
and fans, the flowery bonnets, fancy shoes, purses,
laces, and trims. But today, Felicity studied the shelves.
*Perhaps there is something here that could make my old
brown gown beautiful*, she thought. *Perhaps there is something magic here.* And then Felicity saw the doll.

The doll was standing on a shelf, holding a

bouquet of tiny silk flowers. She had black painted hair
and rosy pink cheeks and an excited expression. *Look at
me!* she seemed to say. Felicity stared. The doll's gown
was made of blue silk. It was the bluest blue there ever
was—bluer than the sky, bluer than the sea—a blue so
bright it lit up the shop. The neck and sleeves of the
gown were trimmed with a frill of lace as white and
delicate as snowflakes. It was the most beautiful gown
Felicity had ever seen.

Oh, if only I could go to the Palace in a gown like that,
thought Felicity. She was so lost in her daydream, she
was surprised when she felt her mother's hand on her
shoulder. Mother stared at the beautiful doll. She was
caught by the doll's magic, too.

"Isn't her gown perfect?" sighed Felicity.

"Aye," said Mrs. Merriman. "But you surprise me,
Felicity. I've never known you to care about gowns and
such before!"

"I've never been invited to the Palace before!"
Felicity burst out. "I've never *needed* a beautiful gown
before!"

"Ah!" said Mrs. Merriman. "I understand."

The milliner took the doll out of the case and handed

it to Felicity with a smile. "I'm quite proud of that gown," she said. "I made it for the doll myself. I copied the pattern from one I saw Lady Dunmore wearing at church. It is the very latest style from England." She held the doll's gown up to Felicity's cheek. "That blue would look lovely with Felicity's pretty red hair, Mrs. Merriman."

"Yes, indeed, it would," said Mother. "But . . ."

"I have the bolt of blue silk right here," said the milliner. "And I have made a lady's-sized pattern for the gown. It would take only a bit of adjusting to make the pattern fit Felicity."

Felicity looked at her mother with a face full of longing.

Suddenly, Mrs. Merriman smiled. "You shall have the beautiful blue gown, Lissie, my dear," she said. "I will make it for you myself."

"Oh, thank you, Mother!" Felicity exclaimed. "Thank you!" She smiled up at her mother and hugged the pretty doll.

"Your father will say I've been foolish," laughed Mother. "But after all, it *is* Christmas. And it's the first gown you've ever *wanted*. Besides, how many times is a

young lady invited to the Governor's Palace? We
will show everyone in Williamsburg how proud we
are of our Lissie. You will look as fashionable as Lady
Dunmore herself!"

The milliner wrapped the blue silk in a tidy parcel.
"I know you are a fine needlewoman, Mrs. Merriman,"
she said. "But if you have any trouble, do please ask me
for help. The finish work may be a bit hard."

Mrs. Merriman looked a little worried. "Oh, dear,"
she said. She tried to stifle a cough with her handkerchief.

"I'll help you, Mother!" Felicity burst out. "At least,
I'll *try*."

Mrs. Merriman handed Felicity the parcel. "We will
both try," she said. "And the gown will be lovely. You
wait and see!"

Felicity was so full of happiness she had no room
for words. She held the precious parcel close to her
chest and smiled at her mother. *I am going to have the
most wonderful gown in all the world,* she thought. *Because
I have the most wonderful mother in all the world!*

That very evening, Mrs. Merriman set to work making Felicity's gown. Felicity watched, biting her bottom

lip with concern, as her mother cut the slippery blue silk into pieces.

"The pieces are such odd shapes, Mother!" Felicity said nervously. "Will they ever come together to make a gown?"

"I do indeed hope so!" Mrs. Merriman smiled. But she looked a little nervous, too. It seemed like a miracle when she pinned the pieces together and Felicity could see sleeves, a waist, and a neckline taking shape.

The next morning, Mrs. Merriman began sewing the pieces together. Felicity was very eager to help. She threaded the needle for her mother and handed her pins as she needed them. She and Nan stood behind Mother's chair, watching her work.

After a little while, Mother turned to them. "Now, girls," she said. "You are making me uncomfortable. Please don't peer over my shoulders and stare at every stitch I make." Then she smiled. "Wouldn't you rather play with the ark?" she asked.

"Yes!" said the girls.

"Me, too!" said William.

"Very well then," said Mother. "Felicity, you may bring it down."

Felicity stood on a stool to lift the ark down from its high shelf. The ark was a special toy they brought out only at Christmastide. All three children loved to play with the wooden boat and the small painted animals that went inside. Now they sat at Mother's feet, happily lining the animals up in pairs.

Every once in a while, Felicity would pop up to check her mother's progress. "Mother," she said, "must you sew so slowly? Couldn't you make bigger stitches? No one is going to see them."

Mrs. Merriman sighed. "Lissie, you know what I always tell you. Haste makes waste. If you want the gown to be perfect, you must be patient."

Patient! It was *always* hard for Felicity to be patient. It was especially hard now, with Christmas only three days away, and the dance lesson at the Palace just thirteen days after that. But as the next few days went by, Felicity tried very hard to be patient. She stood still for hours while her mother fitted the gown to her. It was quite uncomfortable to stand without moving. But Felicity never complained. And when the fittings were over, she tried to help with household chores so that her mother would have more time to work on the gown. She played with William. She read with Nan. She helped Rose in the kitchen. Felicity wanted her mother to have as much time as possible.

Because it was the holiday season, friends and visitors came to call every afternoon. In past years, Felicity had enjoyed all the holiday gaiety. She had fun passing the special Christmas cakes and listening to the visitors' chatter. But this year, Felicity was always impatient for the guests to leave. It seemed to her that they talked on and on and wasted time—time when her mother could have been sewing.

Christmas Eve afternoon brought a steady stream of guests. Felicity's heart sank every time she heard another knock on the door, another hearty voice calling out "Merry Christmas!" She groaned to herself every time another happy, laughing group settled in for a long visit. When the last guests finally left, Felicity sighed with relief. "*Now* you can work on my gown," she said to her mother.

Mrs. Merriman coughed. She looked very tired. "Please, Felicity, don't nag at me," she said. "I have a great deal of work to do to get ready for tomorrow. Run along now!"

Felicity did run along. First she went to Elizabeth's house. Then she and Elizabeth went to the milliner's shop to visit the pretty doll and study every detail of her beautiful gown.

"Your gown will look like that soon," Elizabeth assured her.

"I hope so," said Felicity. "Mother must still attach the sleeves, and do the hem, and add the lace trim . . ."

"Your gown will be finished in time," said Elizabeth. "Don't worry."

The milliner's doll looked as if *she* hadn't a worry in the world. She smiled at Felicity with a cheery smile, full of hope and bright expectations. Felicity felt happier when she looked at the doll.

As soon as she got home, Felicity ran up the stairs. Carefully, she lifted the unfinished gown out of the clothes press. She held the waist of the gown to her own waist. The blue silk swished down around her feet.

"Humph!" someone snorted behind her. Felicity turned and saw Ben. "That fancy gown!" he scoffed. "That's all you care about. You've become a selfish, foolish girl. You think only of dancing at the Palace in your finery, when you think at all. You don't know what is important anymore. If your horse, Penny, came back now, you'd be too busy dreaming to care!"

"That's not true!" cried Felicity.

"I think it is," said Ben. He turned on his heel and left.

Felicity could not sleep that night. She lay awake thinking about what Ben had said. Was she selfish and foolish? She knew she still loved Penny. Could she love dancing and gowns, *too*?

When Felicity heard some rustling downstairs, she crept out of her bedstead and down the stairs. Felicity saw her mother sitting at the table working on the blue gown by the light of a single candle.

"Mother," whispered Felicity. "Why are you working on the gown *now*? The fire is dying and it's dreadfully cold down here."

Mrs. Merriman coughed a bit and smiled a weary smile. "I didn't have time to sew today," she said. "I was busy with guests all afternoon. Then I had to finish decorating. Tomorrow is Christmas."

Felicity looked around the dark parlor. She could see that her mother had decorated every window pane with a cheery sprig of holly. "The parlor looks

beautiful, Mother," said Felicity. She hugged her
mother. "You make *everything* beautiful."

Mrs. Merriman smiled at Felicity as she folded the
blue gown with care. "I love the greenery, too," she
said. "It keeps my spirits up and helps me hold on to
my hopes of spring." She bent to kiss Felicity's forehead.
"And now to bed, Lissie. Tomorrow will be a busy day!"

Christmas Day was full of exciting noises. Cannons
roared and guns were fired to mark the special day.
People called out merry greetings of the season as
Felicity and her family walked to church. Felicity
shivered with pleasure when organ music filled the
church, and everyone's voices soared together as they
sang the joyful songs.

Felicity smiled to herself when the minister read the
words of the Christmas story:

> *And the angel said unto them, Fear not:*
> *for behold I bring good tidings of great joy,*
> *which shall be to all people.*

The words seemed to be meant especially for
Felicity this Christmas. *There,* she thought, *Father is*

right. Christmas is not a time for anger. It is a time of great joy for all people. The angel said so.

There was certainly great joy back at the Merrimans' house when everyone sat down to dinner. Felicity's mother and Rose had prepared a tremendous Christmas feast. Mrs. Merriman sat at the head of the table, serving up steaming bowls of soup and making sure everyone's plate was full of venison, ham, and turkey. She herself cut Ben three pieces of mince pie.

"Rest yourself, my dear," said her husband. "You've stuffed us all and barely taken a bite of the fine feast you and Rose made!" But Mrs. Merriman just smiled and handed around a plate of dates and figs to finish off the glorious meal.

Felicity went to bed full of food and full of happiness. She closed the red-checked curtains around her bedstead so that she would be cozy. She could hear the sweet sound of carolers singing outside beneath her window:

> *Oh, tidings of comfort and joy,*
> *Comfort and joy!*
> *Oh, tidings of comfort and joy!*

Felicity decided there had never been a finer Christmas. As she snuggled under her counterpane and drifted off to sleep, she thought about the beautiful blue gown. *Now that Christmas is over,* she said to herself, *Mother will have time to finish it. That* was a thought of great comfort and great joy.

Gloom and Shadows

hen Felicity awoke the next morning, the
house seemed too quiet, especially after the
jolly noises of the day before. Breakfast was
very odd because Mother was not there.

"Mother is overtired," Father explained. "She wore
herself out making Christmas merry for all of us. She
needs to rest today. But she says she will be up and
about tomorrow."

The day passed slowly. A steady, stubborn rain fell.
Felicity couldn't remember a time when Mother had
stayed in bed all day like this. Several times
Felicity opened the door and peered into the darkness
of Mother's room. *Surely she'll be better tomorrow,* Felicity
thought. *She'll be well enough to sew my gown. The dance
lesson is only twelve days away.*

But Mother was not better the next day, nor the day

after that. In fact, she was much worse. Coughs shook her frail body. She was burning with fever one minute and shivering with chills the next.

Mr. Galt, the apothecary, came to see her. When he walked out of her room, he shook his head and frowned. "She is very ill, Mr. Merriman," he said. "She is so worn down that she has no strength to fight the fever. She is struggling to breathe. I am afraid it looks very bad."

"What can we do?" asked Mr. Merriman. Felicity had never seen him so worried.

"Someone must be with her all the time, both day and night," said Mr. Galt. "Keep the fire in her room bright and warm. If she wakes, try to give her water or broth. I will leave some medicine for you to give her, too."

"But how long will she be this way?" asked Mr. Merriman. "Can't we do any more to help her?"

Mr. Galt paused on his way out the door. "All we can do is to hope and to pray," he said. "We must hope and pray and wait."

From that moment, Felicity's life changed. It was as if she had walked out of the sunlight and into a land

of gloom and shadows, where it was never bright, just
gray all the day long. The outside world did not exist.
No holiday visitors came to call. Felicity did not go to
lessons at Miss Manderly's, or to Elizabeth's house, or
to the milliner's shop to visit the pretty doll.

Felicity, who usually found it hard to sit still for
more than five minutes, now took turns with her father
and Rose, sitting next to her mother's bedside for hours
and hours. She didn't want to be anywhere else. When
her mother shook with chills, Felicity covered her with
blankets. When her mother tossed and turned with
fever, Felicity wiped her forehead with a cool cloth
dipped in lavender scent. Sometimes her mother woke,
but she was too weak to speak. Felicity held a soup
plate of broth to her mother's lips and gave her spoon-
fuls of it. Most of the time, her mother slept a troubled,
uncomfortable, restless sleep.

The days between Christmas and New Year's Day
blurred into one long twilight. When Felicity thought
about the dance lesson at the Palace and the beautiful
blue gown, none of it seemed to matter. There was only
one thing Felicity wanted now. She wanted Mother to
get well.

On New Year's Day, Felicity sat next to her mother's
bed listening to her faint breath. "Happy New Year,
Mother," she whispered. Her mother did not stir.
A cold, cold fear filled Felicity. Her mother's face was
white as the moon. When Mother was well, her hands
were always busy, always moving, always making
things or doing things for others. Now her hands
lay still upon the blankets. Felicity lifted one of her
mother's hands and held it to her own cheek. "I won't
let you die," she whispered. Felicity wished she could
pour some of her own warmth and energy into her
mother. If only she could make Mother well! If only
there were something she could do! But she was help-
less. Felicity put her head down on the bedstead and
cried.

When Felicity came out of Mother's room, Father
was waiting for her. "You have been a great help caring
for Mother," said Father. "I have a New Year's Day
present for you." He smiled as he handed Felicity a
lumpy package wrapped in paper. "Go on!" he said.
"Open it!"

Felicity pulled off the paper and looked at her
present. Her heart twisted. It was the pretty doll from

the milliner's shop, dressed in the glorious blue gown, holding her pink bouquet. Seeing the doll made Felicity feel sad. It reminded her of all that she was missing. But Felicity knew her father meant well. He had given her the doll out of love. She could not bear to let her father know his present made her unhappy. So she smiled as brightly as she could and then hugged her father. "Thank you, Father," she said. "It was very kind of you to get the doll for me. Thank you very much."

Her father looked pleased. "Go along now and play with the doll for a while," he said. "I'll sit with Mother. You need a rest."

"Thank you, Father," she said again. Felicity carried the doll up to her room. She sat on her bed and held the doll at arm's length. Its happy expression seemed empty-headed and foolish to Felicity now. "I was just as foolish as you," Felicity whispered to the doll. "I thought a lot of silly things were important before Mother was sick. I know better now." She touched the doll's cool, silky gown once, then gently hid the doll under her counterpane. She didn't want to see her anymore.

"Felicity!" cried a familiar voice. It was Elizabeth.

She rushed into the room. "How are you? Oh, I have missed you! I do so hope your mother is better. Look, I've brought you a present. It's a blue silk cord to wear around your neck to the dance lesson at the Palace. It will look fine with your gown."

Felicity did not know what to say. She took the blue silk cord from Elizabeth with a sad smile.

"Why, Lissie!" said Elizabeth. "What's the matter?"

"I can't go to the dance lesson at the Palace," Felicity said dully. "My gown cannot be finished in time. And even if it were finished, I wouldn't go. Father needs me to help take care of Mother. Besides, I couldn't possibly feel like dancing when Mother is so ill."

"Lissie!" Elizabeth said fiercely. "You have to go. Your mother would want you to go."

"I don't want to go anymore," said Felicity.

Elizabeth shook her head. "You don't really mean that! Oh, I wish there were something I could do!"

"No one can do anything," said Felicity. She pulled the doll out from under the counterpane.

Elizabeth gasped. "That's the doll from the milliner's shop!"

"Aye," said Felicity. "My father just gave her to me.

I want you to take her. It makes me sad to look at her.
It makes me feel foolish when I remember all the hopes
I had."

Elizabeth gazed at her friend. Her eyes were full
of sorry understanding. At last she said slowly, "Very
well, Lissie. I'll take the doll. I'll keep her for a while.
But I won't let you forget your hopes. Remember what
your father said. Christmas is the time for hopes to
come true."

"I've only one hope now," said Felicity, "and that is
that Mother will get well."

As the long, sad days and nights of the next week
passed, it seemed the rain would never stop. Water
dripped off the roof and muddied the ground. Bare,
rain-wet branches scratched their fingers against the
windows. Felicity was glad the doll was gone. She
didn't want to think about the dance lesson. She never
went to look at her unfinished gown. She knew seeing
it would only make her unhappy.

Mother did not get better. When Felicity was not
caring for Mother, she played with Nan and William.
It was hard to keep them amused when they were
trapped inside every day. But they all liked to play with

the ark. They never tired of putting the animals in the ark, two by two.

"It feels as if we have had rain for forty days and forty nights, just as in Noah's story," Felicity said one day.

"Lissie," said Nan. "God told Noah to gather his family and save two of every animal. But what happened to the animals and the people Noah couldn't fit in his ark?"

"Well, the earth was covered with water," answered Felicity. "So I suppose they drowned."

"What's drowned?" asked William.

"It's when you are all covered with water, and you can't breathe, and so you die," said Nan. "And when you die, that means you go away to heaven forever and never come back. Isn't that right, Lissie?"

"Yes," said Felicity.

"Is Mother going to die and go away and never come back?" asked William.

"No!" said Felicity fiercely. She took William onto her lap to comfort him. "No," she said again, more gently. "Mother won't die. She will be well again. The rain will stop. All will be fine again, just as it was in the

Noah story. Remember? The rain finally stopped. Noah sent a bird out of the ark. The bird came back with a sprig of leaves in its mouth, so Noah knew somewhere there was land."

Felicity broke a little holly leaf off one of the garlands her mother had made. It was stiff and dry, but it was still green. She gave the leaf to William. "Just think how happy Noah must have been to see a green leaf like this," she said. "The leaf showed him that everything would be all right. It gave him hope."

Nan and William looked at Felicity trustingly. *They need me to be brave,* she thought. So she grinned. "Put the leaf in our ark, William," she said. "Then our Noah will be happy, too."

William lifted the roof of the ark and put the leaf inside.

Felicity looked around the parlor. Most of the Christmas decorations were growing dry and brown. "I know what we should do!" she said. "We must pull down all these dying decorations. We'll make new ones that are fresh and green. That way, when Mother wakes up, the house will look cheery. *We'll* make some New Year's magic for Mother. Won't that be fine?"

"Yes!" said Nan and William, excited for the first time in a long while.

"Good, then!" said Felicity. She pulled a brittle sprig of holly off one of the windows and tossed it onto the fire. "Let's begin!"

A Season for Surprises

elicity leaned forward so that the sleet would not sting her face. She'd had a long afternoon of errands and was scurrying home from her last stop at the apothecary shop with more medicine for her mother. She was buried so deep in her hood, she jumped when she heard a coachman call out, "Stand away, missie!"

She stepped back just in time. Muddy-legged horses trotted by, pulling a carriage through a puddle right in front of her. The wheels of the carriage splashed her petticoat with slush. The carriage hastened on, headed toward the Palace. Suddenly Felicity remembered, *Today is January seventh, the day of the dance lesson at the Palace.*

Felicity shivered. She headed home, cold and wet and miserable.

Felicity hung up her cloak and slipped off her muddy shoes. Her father beckoned her into the parlor. "Come here, Felicity," he said softly.

Felicity's heart thudded. "What is it, Father?" she asked. "Is Mother all right?"

Mr. Merriman smiled. "Come see for yourself!" he said.

Felicity looked behind him. "Mother!" she gasped. Mrs. Merriman was propped comfortably in a big chair next to the fire, cocooned in pillows and blankets. Nan, William, and Ben stood around her. She smiled and opened her arms to Felicity.

Felicity ran to her mother and hugged her gently. "Oh, Mother," she said. "Oh, I'm so *glad*." Felicity wanted to stay in the circle of her mother's arms forever.

"The fever is gone," said Father. "Her cough is still bad, and she is very weak. But at last she is starting to get better."

"I am indeed, thanks to you, Lissie, my good nurse," said Mother. Her voice was hoarse but full of happiness. "You've taken good care of me. Father tells me that you've taken good care of William and Nan, too. Thank you, my dear girl."

"We made new decorations for you, Mother," said
Nan. "Lissie did most of the work. But William and I
helped, too."

"The parlor looks beautiful," said Mrs. Merriman.
"It makes me feel better just to see all that lovely,
fresh greenery. What a nice surprise! You truly are my
Christmas sprites!" She smiled at Felicity. "Perhaps we
could all have a cup of chocolate to celebrate."

"Certainly, my dear," said Mr. Merriman.

"I'll make the chocolate!" said Felicity.

"First you must go and change your clothes," said
Mr. Merriman. "You are wet through to the skin. We
mustn't have *you* fall sick. Go along now."

Felicity hugged her mother once more, then turned
and picked up a chamberstick to light her way up
the stairs. *Mother is better! Mother is better!* her heart
sang. Felicity felt as if her dearest wish had come true.
The cold fear that had haunted her melted away into
happiness and relief. *Mother is going to be all right! She
really and truly will be all right!*

When Felicity reached the door of her room, she
stopped stock still. She could not believe her eyes.
The beautiful blue gown was spread out on her bed,

glowing in the light of her candle. Every stitch was perfectly finished. Was it magic?

Felicity touched it to be sure it was real. The blue silk was as smooth and soft as a sigh, but it was very real.

How could this be? Felicity wondered. *Who finished the gown?* Then she noticed the pretty doll in its matching blue gown sitting upon her pillow. The doll's eyes were bright, and she looked even more cheery and pleased with herself than usual. "Elizabeth!" gasped Felicity. Could she have done it? *Oh, Elizabeth, thank you!* Felicity thought.

Carefully, Felicity lifted the gown in her arms and hurried downstairs to the parlor where her family and Ben were still gathered.

Mother sat forward in her chair. "Felicity!" she gasped. "You have your gown! Your heavenly blue gown! Did *you* finish it?"

"No," said Felicity. "Elizabeth must have!" Felicity held the gown against herself and swirled around. The blue silk glowed in the light of the fire and brightened the parlor. "Isn't it the prettiest gown you've ever seen?"

"Aye," said Mrs. Merriman. "It is."

Mr. Merriman smiled sadly. "I'm so sorry you can't show off your gown as it deserves. I know this is the day of the dance lesson. But I don't know how you can be properly taken to the Palace. Rose isn't here, and I can't leave your mother. You cannot possibly arrive alone. And there is no one else to escort you."

"I understand," said Felicity quietly.

A shadow of sadness crossed Mrs. Merriman's face. She reached out to stroke the glorious blue silk of Felicity's gown.

Suddenly Ben spoke up. "I'll do it," he said. "I'll escort Felicity to the Palace."

Felicity stared at Ben. "But, but Ben . . ." she began. "I thought you . . ." She was too confused and happy to go on.

Mr. Merriman laughed and nodded at Ben with a pleased expression. "Good lad!" he said. He turned to Felicity. "You had better hurry and get ready, Lissie, my dear. 'Tis already nearly four."

Ben was halfway out the door. "I'll get the riding chair ready and bring it around to the front," he said.

Mrs. Merriman's cheeks were pink with excitement.

"Edward," she said to Mr. Merriman, "please bring a bathing tub and some buckets of hot water in from the kitchen. Lissie must have a bath. William, fetch some of my very best soap and a linen cloth. Nan, bring the hairbrush. Make haste! We must get Lissie ready to go to the Palace."

Before Felicity knew it, she was scrubbed clean. Her skin glowed pink and smelled of roses. Nan brushed her hair till it was smooth and shiny as copper. As if in a dream, Felicity slipped the blue silk gown over her head. It fit perfectly. Felicity had never felt so beautiful in her life. Her hands shook a little as she tied the blue cord around her neck. Mother studied her with a loving eye. "Nan," she said. "Run and fetch one of my best pearl earrings from the case in my drawer."

Nan hurried to her mother's room and was soon back with the earring. Mother fastened the earring on the blue silk cord around Felicity's neck. "There," said Mother, "there." She sank back into the pillows, looking pleased and proud. "Now you look perfect. Off you go."

Felicity gave her mother one last hug, then pulled on her cloak and rushed outside to meet Ben. It was still sleeting, and the roads were rutted and slippery. But Ben hurried Old Bess along and pulled up to the Palace gates in no time.

Felicity held tight to Ben's hand as he helped her down from the riding chair. She felt rather small when she looked up at the tall iron gates in the wall around the Palace. Tonight the gates were open wide. Inside them, a row of lanterns lit the path up to the Palace doors. At the doors, Ben gave her hand a squeeze. "Thank you, Ben," she whispered. Ben grinned and disappeared behind her.

Felicity held her breath as she was shown into the Palace entry hall by a footman. The entry hall was big and a little scary. The walls and even the ceiling were covered with fierce-looking swords, pistols, and muskets glinting in the candlelight. Another footman took her wet cloak.

On wobbly legs, Felicity walked the length of the ballroom. A very elegant lady and gentleman stood at the far end under huge portraits of the king and queen. Felicity's heart thumped when she realized, *This must be Lord and Lady Dunmore!* She sank into a blue cloud of silk as she made her curtsy. "My lord. My lady," she murmured, just as she and Elizabeth had practiced so many times. "I have the honor to be Miss Felicity Merriman."

"Miss Merriman," said Lady Dunmore. "How charming! We are so glad you have come to join the others. I believe they are about to begin the lesson."

"Thank you," said Felicity as she rose.

The ballroom was a dazzling blue. Felicity's eyes opened wide in amazement. She'd never seen such a huge room in all her life! It was lit with dozens of candles glittering in chandeliers. *Oh, if only Mother could see this,* she thought. The room was full of young gentlemen dressed in bright silk breeches and coats decorated with gold braid and rows of buttons. Young ladies blossomed like flowers in brocades and taffetas, silks and velvets of every color. *Ah, but my gown is the loveliest,* thought Felicity happily.

Felicity looked around the room. At last she caught sight of Elizabeth and hurried toward her. But just as she reached her friend, the music began. Felicity found herself part of a set of dancers. Elizabeth beamed at her, but they had no chance to talk, for they were soon swept into the music and dancing. The dance master called out the dances. Felicity knew she had better pay close attention. She did not want to make any mistakes!

The beautiful blue gown worked its magic. As the dance lesson went on, Felicity felt more and more at ease. She did not trip, or step on anyone's toes. In fact, she began to enjoy the dances. The blue gown seemed to help her swoop and swirl and stay light on her feet. *Why, dancing is fun!* she thought with surprise.

And when the dancing was over, the young ladies and gentlemen were invited to take refreshments in the supper room. Felicity had never seen such elegant food! There were towers of sweetmeats and sugared fruits. There were plates of cakes and tarts. Bowls of punch and platters of jellies crowded the long table. It all seemed too beautiful to eat. And Felicity was too excited to be hungry. Besides, she couldn't wait to talk to Elizabeth.

"Elizabeth!" she called. She hurried over to her friend through the throng of people. "You did it, didn't you?" She held out her skirts and twirled. "You finished my gown. But *how* ever did you do it?"

Elizabeth smiled. "My mother did the hardest parts, but I helped her. Even Annabelle helped," she said.

"It looks beautiful, doesn't it?"

Felicity smoothed the blue silk skirts and looked at Elizabeth. "How can I thank you and your mother and Annabelle?" she said. "Oh, Elizabeth! You kept hoping even after I had given up. No one ever had a better friend than you!"

"You have another good friend," Elizabeth said with a grin. "Ben helped me. He sneaked the gown out of your house and then back in again."

"Ben?" asked Felicity. "But he thought the gown was foolish. And he thought it was wrong for me to come to the Palace! How did you change his mind?"

Elizabeth shrugged happily. "I just asked him to help."

"Did you ask Ben to escort me here tonight?" asked Felicity.

"No," smiled Elizabeth. "But I am very glad he did!"

"I am, too," sighed Felicity happily. "I am, too."

When the dance lesson was over, the girls said their thank-yous and their good-nights. Felicity wrapped herself in her cloak as she stepped outside the Palace. It was as if all the beauty from the ballroom had spilled

out into the night. A fine, cool white powdering of
snow had come silently, making the world sparkle.
Now the clouds were clearing. For the first time in a
long time, Felicity could look up at the stars. The moon
lit the clouds from behind so that they were outlined
in silver.

Ben was waiting for Felicity outside the Palace
gates. She climbed into the riding chair and sat next to
him. They rode in silence for a while. Then Felicity said,
"Ben, it was kind of you to help Elizabeth. And it was
kind of you to escort me to the Palace. What made you
change your mind?"

A wonderful smile lit up Ben's face. "You did," he
said. "I watched you take care of your mother. I saw
how you cheered Nan and William even when all of the
things you had hoped for looked impossible. I began to
think your father was right. Christmas *is* the time when
our hopes for peace and happiness should come true.
I wanted to help your hopes come true, too."

"Thank you, Ben," said Felicity. They rode home
together in the silvery night.

INSIDE Felicity's World

Felicity was born in Virginia, which today is one of the 50 states in the United States of America. In 1774, Virginia was one of the 13 colonies ruled by King George III in England. A *colony* is a group of people who settle in a new land but follow a different country's laws. Thousands of people from Europe and Africa had come to America. Some were brought against their will as slaves, while others eagerly crossed the ocean in hope of a better life, a chance to own land, or the opportunity to worship freely.

When Felicity was a young girl, most Virginia families lived on farms, but some lived in towns. Williamsburg was the capital of the colony, and its residents were proud of their city. They liked things to be elegant, graceful, and orderly. Homes were neat and tidy, and gardens were arranged in beautiful patterns. The Merrimans' garden was as pretty as it was useful. Felicity's family grew sweet-smelling flowers along with vegetables and herbs.

Felicity learned a great deal at home, including how to read and write. There were few schools during Felicity's time. Children from wealthy families often had a *tutor*, a young man with some college education who lived in the family's house and taught the children. Sometimes the boys, but not the girls, then went to a grammar school where they learned subjects such as geography, Greek, and Latin. Some teenage boys and girls became apprentices like Ben, learning to become shopkeepers or craftspeople by working for a merchant, blacksmith, or wig maker.

Girls like Felicity were given a very different education. People thought girls didn't need to study ideas in books, since they were expected to marry and to run a home. Instead, mothers taught their daughters to cook, sew, and preserve food. Often girls were sent to teachers like Miss Manderly to learn to dance, play musical instruments, and practice fancy stitchery. They were also taught the proper way to serve tea. At tea lessons, they practiced their manners and learned to carry on polite conversation.

In 1774, conversations all over Williamsburg had turned to the rumors of war. People talked about the ways the king of England treated the colonists. Patriots, like Felicity's father, did not think it was fair to pay taxes to the king for things like tea that they bought in America. They agreed that the colonies should be independent from England. Loyalists, like Elizabeth's father, thought it was wrong to go against the king and still wanted the colonies to be under his rule.

Felicity had an important choice to make. To support her father and the Patriots, she had to refuse to drink tea at Miss Manderly's. But the tea ceremony was an important part of her education as a gentlewoman, and she did not want to offend her teacher. By politely turning her cup upside down and saying "I shall take no tea," Felicity expressed her beliefs about loyalty, independence, and freedom.

Read more of FELICITY'S stories,

available from booksellers and at *americangirl.com*

❧ *Classics* ❧

Felicity's classic series, now in two volumes:

Volume 1:
Love and Loyalty
When Felicity falls in love with a beautiful horse, she takes a great risk to save the mare from her cruel owner.

Volume 2:
A Stand for Independence
Felicity's friend Ben has run off to join the army. Now he needs her help—in secret. Should Felicity break Ben's trust?

❧ *Journey in Time* ❧

Travel back in time—and spend a day with Felicity!

Gunpowder and Tea Cakes

Experience the American Revolution with Felicity! Ride horses, visit the Governor's Palace—or get involved in a gunpowder plot! Choose your own path through this multiple-ending story.

❧ *Mysteries* ❧

More thrilling adventures with Felicity!

Peril at King's Creek

Felicity is having a wonderful summer at her grandfather's plantation, until she discovers the farm—and her horse—are in danger!

Traitor in Williamsburg

Father has been accused of being a traitor! When he is arrested, Felicity must find out who is behind the terrible accusation.

Lady Margaret's Ghost

Felicity doesn't believe in ghosts . . . until odd and eerie things begin to happen after a mysterious package arrives.

A Sneak Peek at

A Stand for Independence

A Felicity Classic

Volume 2

Felicity's adventures continue in the
second volume of her classic stories.

One summer afternoon, as Felicity was riding one of Grandfather's horses from the stable to the upper pasture, she passed Nan and William. They had reeds, and shells full of soapy water, and they were blowing bubbles up into the branches of a large, old shade tree.

"Lissie," said William, "when you pass the bird bottle, do remember to look inside it. Maybe a bird has built a nest today."

Felicity and Nan looked at each other and sighed. William asked Felicity to look in the bird bottle almost every day, even though both girls had told him a hundred times that birds don't build nests in the summer. "William," said Nan patiently, "you and Lissie looked yesterday. There is no nest in the bottle. There never is. There never is *anything* in the bottle."

William ignored Nan. "You'll look, won't you, Lissie? Promise?"

"I promise," said Felicity quickly. She was impatient to go. She nudged the horse, and they trotted away. As they passed the smokehouse, Felicity glanced at the bird bottle to keep her promise to William, even though she knew nothing would be there.

But to her great surprise, Felicity saw something white in the bird bottle. She reined the horse to a stop and squinted at it. Was the sun playing tricks on her eyes? Felicity rode up for a closer look.

There *was* something there. It was a scrap of cloth. Felicity put her hand in the bird bottle and pulled the cloth out. It looked like the corner of a handkerchief. It was wrapped around something hard, something like a stick. Quickly, Felicity unrolled the cloth. Out fell a wooden whistle. Felicity stared at it. She knew it was a signal whistle because she had seen Ben's. He had shown her how to blow it, and how it was used to give commands to soldiers. In fact, this signal whistle looked exactly like Ben's. Whose was it? Why had someone put it in the bird bottle? Why was it wrapped in a scrap of handkerchief that was stained with berry juice?

Felicity looked at the stains more closely and gasped. They were not stains at all! They were words, written with a stick dipped in berry juice! Felicity read the words on the scrap of cloth:

Felicity, Come! Help!
—Ben

Ben? Ben was supposed to be in Williamsburg. How could he have left this note for her? Where was he? If he was nearby, why didn't he come to her grandfather's house? And why did he need her help? Felicity's mind was spinning.

Below the words on the scrap of cloth, Ben had made a rough map. The map showed Grandfather's house, the river, and the woods. There was an X in the woods. That must be where Ben was.

Felicity took a shaky breath. Suddenly, it was all clear to her. Ben was hiding. For some reason, he didn't want anyone but her to know where he was. Ben wanted her to find him by following the map. She should blow his signal whistle so that he would know it was safe to show himself. Felicity did not stop to think anymore. She urged the horse to a trot and went to look for Ben in the woods.

Felicity entered the woods just behind the blackberry thicket. When she was deep in the forest, Felicity blew the signal whistle once, twice, three times. She heard Ben whistle in reply, and she rode toward the sound. It was not hard to find him, though he was well away from the riding path. He sat propped up against a big tree. One leg was stretched out in front of him, wrapped in bloody rags.

"Ben!" exclaimed Felicity. "Benjamin Davidson! What on earth are you doing here?" She slipped off the horse. "What's happened to you?"

Ben groaned and closed his eyes. Felicity stopped talking. She knelt next to him and then said quietly, "Ben, tell me what you are doing."

Ben opened his eyes. His face was sweaty and streaked with mud. "I ran away," he said. "You know I want to be a soldier and fight with the Patriots. Two companies of soldiers from Virginia have already marched to Massachusetts to join the army George Washington is gathering there." Ben took a deep breath. "It's starting, Lissie," he said. "General Washington is going to lead an army of Patriots. We're going to fight the British. We're going to overthrow the rule of the king here in the colonies. I want to be part of the fight. But my apprenticeship agreement with your father won't allow it. So," he repeated, "I ran away."

"When?" asked Felicity.

"The night before last," answered Ben. "I thought I could make it to the Yorktown ferry and cross the river before your father . . . before I was missed."

Felicity sighed. "What went wrong?" she asked.

"I knew I couldn't walk along the main road for fear of being seen," said Ben. "Still, I made good time through the woods until I came to King's Creek. It was so dark, I slipped and fell when I was crossing the creek. I lost my pack of clothes and food and money. And I cut my leg on a sharp branch."

"Your leg looks bad," said Felicity. "It must hurt."

Ben shrugged. "I knew I was not far from your grandfather's plantation, and I knew I needed your help. I found my way here and slept by this tree. Yesterday, I sneaked up closer to the house. I saw you and William looking at the bird bottle. So last night, I wrote you that message and hid it with my whistle in the bird bottle. I was hoping you'd find them today. I am very glad you did."

"I'm glad, too," said Felicity. She stood up and dusted off her gown. "Because now I can tell you how foolish I think you're being. I'm going straight up to the house to fetch Grandfather."

Ben reached up and grabbed Felicity's arm. "Don't!" he said. "Your grandfather is a Loyalist. He thinks the

Patriots are wrong. You can't tell him about me, Lissie!"

Felicity yanked her arm away. "Yes, I can!" she said. "I'd be dishonest if I didn't. I can't keep a secret like this!" She stalked away and swung herself up onto her grandfather's horse. She turned to take one last look down at Ben. He was solemn. Suddenly, Felicity remembered how Ben had helped her keep a secret last fall. Ben had never told Mother or Father that Felicity was sneaking off every morning to ride Penny. She had asked Ben to keep her secret, and he had. How could she not do the same for him?

Felicity spoke slowly. "Very well, Ben," she said. "I promise I will not tell anyone about you. You can trust me. I'll go back to the house now. But I'll be back soon with food and water and some medicine for your leg. Rest easy. I won't be long." She smiled at Ben a little bit. "You kept my secret. I shall keep yours. I promise."

Ben grinned for the first time. "I knew you would, Felicity," he said. "You are a faithful friend."

About the Author

VALERIE TRIPP says that she became a writer because of the kind of person she is. She says she's curious, and writing requires you to be interested in everything. Talking is her favorite sport, and writing is a way of talking on paper. She's a daydreamer, which helps her come up with her ideas. And she loves words. She even loves the struggle to come up with just the right words as she writes and rewrites. Ms. Tripp lives in Maryland with her husband.